The Prelude to Adventure by Hugh Walpole

Sir Hugh Seymour Walpole, CBE was born in Auckland, New Zealand, on March 13th, 1884.

His parents had moved to New Zealand in 1877, but his mother, Mildred, unable to settle there, eventually persuaded her husband, Somerset, an Anglican clergyman, to accept another post, this time in New York in 1889. Walpole's early years involved being educated by a Governess until, in 1893, his parents decided he needed an English education and the young Walpole was sent to England.

He first attended a preparatory school in Truro. He naturally missed his family but was reasonably happy. A move to Sir William Borlase's Grammar School in Marlow in 1895, found him bullied, frightened and miserable.

The following year, 1897, the Walpole's returned to England and Walpole was moved to be a day boy at Durham School. His sense of isolation increased. His refuge was the local library and reading.

From 1903 to 1906 Walpole studied history at Emmanuel College, Cambridge and there, in 1905, had his first work published, the critical essay "Two Meredithian Heroes".

Walpole was also attempting to cope with and come to terms with his homosexual feelings and to find "that perfect friend".

After a short spell tutoring in Germany and then teaching French at Epsom in 1908 he found the desire to fully immerse himself in the literary world. He moved to London to become a book reviewer for The Standard and to write fiction in his spare time. In 1909, he published his first novel, The Wooden Horse. The book received good reviews but sold little.

Better was to come in 1911 when he published Mr Perrin and Mr Traill. In early 1914 Henry James wrote an article for The Times Literary Supplement surveying the younger generation of British novelists. Walpole was greatly encouraged that one of the greatest living authors had publicly ranked him among the finest young British novelists.

As war approached, Walpole realised that his poor eyesight would disqualify him from service and accepted an appointment, based in Moscow, reporting for The Saturday Review and The Daily Mail. Although allowed to visit the front in Poland, these dispatches were not enough to stop hostile comments at home that he was not 'doing his bit' for the war effort.

Walpole was ready with a counter; an appointment as a Russian officer, in the Sanitar. He explained they were "part of the Red Cross that does the rough work at the front, carrying men out of the trenches, helping at the base hospitals in every sort of way, doing every kind of rough job".

During a skirmish in June 1915 Walpole rescued a wounded soldier; his Russian comrades refused to help and this meant Walpole had to carry one end of a stretcher, dragging the man to safety. He was awarded the Cross of Saint George. By late 1917 it was clear to Walpole, and the authorities, that his work was at an end. In London Walpole joined the Foreign Office and remained there until resigning in February 1919. For his wartime work he was awarded the CBE in 1918.

Walpole continued to write and publish and now also began a career on the highly lucrative lecture tour in the United States.

In 1924 Walpole moved to a house, Brackenburn, near Keswick in the Lake District. Although he maintained a flat in Piccadilly, Brackenburn was to be his main home for the rest of his life.

At the end of 1924 Walpole met Harold Cheevers, who soon became his friend and constant companion and remained so for the rest of his life; "that perfect friend".

Hollywood, in the shape of MGM, invited him in 1934 to write the script for a film of David Copperfield. He also had a small acting role in the film.

In 1937 Walpole was offered a knighthood. He accepted although Kipling, Hardy, Galsworthy had all refused. "I'm not of their class... Besides I shall like being a knight," he said.

Unfortunately his health was undermined by diabetes made worse by the frenetic pace of his life. Sir Hugh Seymour Walpole, CBE died of a heart attack at Brackenburn, aged 57 on June 1st, 1941. He was buried in St John's churchyard in Keswick.

Index of Contents

CHAPTER I

LAST CHAPTER

"There is a God after all." That was the immense conviction that faced him as he heard, slowly, softly, the leaves, the twigs, settle themselves after that first horrid crash which the clumsy body had made.

Olva Dune stood for an instant straight and stiff, his arms heavily at his side, and the dank, misty wood slipped back once more into silence. There was about him now the most absolute stillness: some trees dripped in the mist; far above him, on the top of the hill, the little path showed darkly—below him, in the hollow, black masses of fern and weed lay heavily under the chill November air—at his feet there was the body.

In that sudden after silence he had known beyond any question that might ever again arise, that there was now a God—God had watched him.

With grave eyes, with hands that did not tremble, he surveyed and then, bending, touched the body. He knelt in the damp, heavy soil, tore open the waistcoat, the shirt; the flesh was yet warm to his touch—the heart was still. Carfax was dead.

It had happened so instantly. First that great hulking figure in front of him, the sneering laugh, that last sentence, "Let her rot . . . my dear Dune, your chivalry does you credit." Then that black, blinding, surging rage and the blow that followed. He did not know what he had intended to do. It did not matter—only in the force that there had been in his arm there had been the accumulated hatred of years, hatred that dated from that first term at school thirteen years ago when he had known Carfax for the dirty hypocrite that he was. He could not stay now to think of the many things that had led to this climax. He only knew that as he raised himself again from the body there was with him no feeling of repentance, no suggestion of fear, only a grim satisfaction that he had struck so hard, and, above all, that lightning certainty that he had had of God.

His brain was entirely alert. He did not doubt, as he stood there, that he would be caught and delivered and hanged. He, himself, would take no steps to prevent such a catastrophe. He would leave the body there as it was: to-night, to-morrow they would find it,—the rest would follow. He was, indeed, acutely interested in his own sensations. Why was it that he felt no fear? Where was the terror that followed, as he had so often heard, upon murder? Why was it that the dominant feeling in him should be that at last he had justified his existence? In that furious blow there had leapt within him the creature that he had always been—the creature subdued, restrained, but always there—there through all this civilized existence; the creature that his father was, that his grandfather, that all his ancestors, had been. He looked down. The hulking body that had been Carfax made a hollow in the wet and broken fern. The face was white, stupid, the cheeks hanging fat, horrible, the eyes staring. One leg was twisted beneath the body. Still in the air there seemed to linger that startled little cry—"Oh!"—surprise, wonder—and then fading miserably into nothing as the great body fell.

Such a huge hulking brute; now so sordid and useless, looking at last, after all these years, the thing that it ought always to have looked. Some money had rolled from the pocket and lay shining amongst the fern. A gold ring glittered on the white finger, seeming in the heart of that silence the only living note.

Then Olva remembered his dog—where was he? He turned and saw the fox terrier down on all fours amongst the fern, motionless, his tongue out, his eyes gazing with animal inquiry at his master. The dog was waiting for the order to continue the walk. He seemed, in his passivity, merely to be resting, a little exhausted perhaps by the heavy closeness of the day, too indolent to nose amongst the leaves for possible adventure: Olva looked at him. The dog caught the look and beat the grass with his tail, soft, friendly taps to show that he only waited for orders. Then still idly, still with that air of gentle amusement, the dog gazed at the thing in the grass. He rose slowly and very delicately advanced a few steps: for an instant some fear seemed to strike his heart for he stopped suddenly and gazed into his master's face for reassurance. What he saw there comforted him. Again he wagged his tail placidly and half closed his eyes in sleepy indifference.

Then Olva, without another backward glance, left the hollow, crashed through the fern up the hill and struck the little brown path. Bunker, the dog, pattered patiently behind him.

II

Olva Dune was twenty-three years of age. He was of Spanish descent, and it was only within the last two generations that English blood had mingled with the Dune stock. He was of no great height, slim and dark. His hair was black, his complexion sallow, and on his upper lip he wore a small dark moustache. His ears were small, his mouth thin, his chin sharply pointed, but his eyes, large, dark brown, were his best feature. They were eyes that looked as though they held in their depths the possibility of tenderness. He walked as an athlete, there was no spare flesh about him anywhere, and in his carriage there was a dignity that had in it pride of birth, complete self-possession, and above all, contempt for his fellow-creatures.

He despised all the world save only his father. He had gone through his school-life and was now passing through his college-life as a man travels through a country that has for him no interest and no worth but that may lead, once it has been traversed, to something of importance and adventure. He was now at the beginning of his second year at Cambridge and was regarded by every one with distrust, admiration, excitement. His was one of the more interesting personalities at that time in residence at Saul's.

He had come with a historical scholarship and a great reputation as a Three-quarter from Rugby. He was considered to be a certain First Class and a certain Rugby Blue; he, lazily and indifferently during the course of his first term, discouraged both these anticipations. He attended no lectures, received a Third Class in his May examinations, and was deprived of his scholarship at the end of his first year. He played brilliantly in the Freshmen's Rugby match, but so indolently in the first University match of the season that he was not invited again. Had he played merely badly he would have been given a second trial, but his superior insolence was considered insulting. He never played in any College matches nor did he trouble to watch any of their glorious conflicts. Once and again he produced an Essay for his Tutor that astonished that gentleman very considerably, but when called before the Dean for neglecting to attend lectures explained that he was studying the Later Roman Empire and could not possibly attend to more than one thing at a time.

He was perfectly friendly to every one, and it was curious that, with his air of contempt for the world in general, he had made no enemies. He wondered at that himself, on occasions; he had always been supposed, for instance, to be very good friends with Carfax. He had, of course, always hated Carfax—and now Carfax was dead.

The little crooked path soon left the dark wood and merged into the long white Cambridge road. The flat country was veiled in mist, only, like a lantern above a stone wall, the sun was red over the lower veils of white that rose from the sodden fields. Some trees started like spies along the road. Overhead, where the mists were faint, the sky showed the faintest of pale blue. The long road rang under Olva's step—it would be a frosty night.

When the little wood was now a black ball in the mist Olva was suddenly sick. He leant against one of the dark mysterious trees and was wretchedly, horribly ill. Slowly, then, the colour came back to his cheeks, his hands were once more steady, he could see again clearly. He addressed the strange world about him, the long flat fields, the hard white road, the orange sun. "That is the last time," he said aloud, "the last weakness."

He definitely braced himself to face life. There would not be much of it—to-morrow he would be arrested: meanwhile there should be no more of these illusions. There was, for instance, the illusion that the body was following him, bounding grotesquely along the hard road. He knew that again and again he turned his head to see whether anything were there, and the further the little wood was left behind the nearer did the body seem to be. He must not allow himself to think these things. Carfax was dead—Carfax was dead—Carfax was dead. It was a good thing that Carfax was dead. He had saved, he hoped, Rose Midgett—that at any rate he had done; it was a good thing for Rose Midgett that he had killed Carfax. He had, incidentally, no interest on his own account in Rose Midgett—he scarcely knew her by sight—but it was pleasant to think that she would be no longer worried. . . .

Then there was that question about God. Now the river appeared, darkly, dimly below the road, the reeds rising spire-like towards the faint blue sky. That question about God—Olva had never believed in any kind of a God. His father had defied God and the Devil time and again and had been none the worse for it. And yet—here and there about the world people lived and had their being to whom this question of God was a vital question; people like Bunning and his crowd—mad, the whole lot of them. Nevertheless there was something there that had great power. That had, until to-day, been Olva's attitude, an amused superior curiosity.

Now it was a larger question. There had been that moment after Carfax had fallen, a moment of intense silence, and in that moment something had spoken to Olva. It is a fact as sure as concrete, as though he himself could remember words and gesture. There had been Something there. . . .

Brushing this for an instant aside, he faced next the question of his arrest. There was no one, save his father, for whom he need think. He would send his father word saying—"I have killed a beast—fairly—in the open"—that would be all.

He would not be hanged—poison should see to that. Dunes had murdered, raped, tortured—never yet had they died on the gallows.

And now, for the first time, the suspicion crossed his mind that perhaps, after all, he might escape—escape, at any rate, that order of punishment. Here on this desolate road, he had met no living soul; the mists encompassed him and they had now swallowed the dripping wood and all that it contained. It had always been supposed that he was good friends with Carfax, as good friends as he allowed himself to be with any one. No one had known in which direction he would take his walk; he had come upon Carfax entirely by chance. It might quite naturally be supposed that some tramp had attempted robbery. To the world at large Olva could have had no possible motive. But, for the moment, these thoughts were dismissed. It seemed to him just now immaterial whether he lived or died. Life had not hitherto been so wonderful a discovery that the making of it had been entirely worth while. He had no tenor of disgrace; his father was his only court of appeal, and that old rocky sinner, sitting alone with his proud spirit and his grey hairs, in his northern fastness, hating and despising the world, would himself slay, had he the opportunity, as many men of the Carfax kind as he could find. He had no terror of pain—he did not know what that kind of fear was. The Dunes had always faced Death.

But he began, dimly, now to perceive that there were larger, crueller issues before him than these material punishments. He had known since he was a tiny child a picture by some Spanish painter, whose name he had forgotten, that had always hung on the wall of the passage opposite his bedroom. It was a large engraving in sharply contrasted black and white, of a knight who rode through mists along a climbing road up into the heart of towering hills. The mountains bad an active life in the picture; they seemed to crowd forward eager to swallow him. Beside the spectre horse that he rode there was no other life. The knight's face, white beneath his black helmet, was tired and worn. About him was the terror of loneliness.

From his earliest years this idea of loneliness had pleasantly seized upon Olva's mind. His father had always impressed upon him that the Dunes had ever been lonely—lonely in a world that was contemptible. He had always until now accepted this idea and found it confirmed on every side. His six years at Rugby had encouraged him—he had despised, with his tolerant smile, boys and masters alike; all insincere, all weak, all to be used, if he wanted them, as he chose to use them. He had thought often of the lonely knight—that indeed should be his attitude to the world.

But now, suddenly, as the scattered Cambridge houses with their dull yellow lights began to creep stealthily through the mist, upon the road, he knew for the first time that loneliness could be terrible. He was hurrying now, although he had not formerly been conscious of it, hurrying into the lights and comforts and noise of the town. There might only be for him now a night and day of freedom, but, during that time, he must not, he must not be alone. The patter of Bunker's feet beside him pleased him. Bunker was now a fact of great importance to him.

And now he could see further. He could see that he must always now, from the consciousness of the thing that he had done, he alone. The actual moment of striking his blow had put an impassable gulf between his soul and all the world. Bodies might touch, hands might be grasped, voices ring together, always now his soul must be alone. Only, that Something—of whose Presence he had been, in that instant, aware—could keep his company. They two . . . they two. . . .

The suburbs of Cambridge had closed about him. Those dreary little streets, empty as it seemed of all life, facing him sullenly with their sodden little yellow lamps, shivering, grumbling, he could fancy, in the chill of that November evening, eyed him with suspicion. He walked through them now, with his shoulders back, his head up. He could fancy how, to-morrow, their dull placidity would be wrung by the discovery of the crime. The little wood would fling its secret into the eager lap of these decrepit witches; they would crowd to their doors, chatter it, shout it, pull it to pieces. "Body of an Undergraduate . . . Body of an Undergraduate. . . ."

He turned out of their cold silence over the bridge that spanned the river, up the path that crossed the common into the heart of the town, Here, at once, he was in the hubbub. The little streets were mediaeval in their narrow space, in their cobbles, in the old black, fantastic walls that hung above them. Beauty, too, on this November evening, shone through the misty lamplight. Beauty in the dark purple of the evening sky, beauty in the sudden vista of grey courts with lighted windows, like eyes, seen through stone gateways. Beauty in the sudden golden shadows of some corner shop glittering through the mist; beauty in the overshadowing of the many towers that were like grey clouds in mid-air.

The little streets chattered with people—undergraduates in Norfolk jackets, grey flannel trousers short enough to show the brightest of socks, walked arm in arm—voices rang out—men called across the streets—hansoms rattled like little whirlwinds along the cobbles—many bells were ringing—dark bodies, leaning from windows, gave uncouth cries . . . over it all the mellow lamplight.

Into this happy confusion Olva Dune plunged. He shook off from him, as a dog shakes water from his back, the memory of that white mist-haunted road. Once he deliberately faced the moment when he had been sick—faced it, heard once again the dull, lumbering sound that the body had made as it bundled along the road, and then put it from him altogether. Now for battle . . . his dark eyes challenged this shifting cloud of life.

He went round to the stable where Bunker was housed, chattered with the blue-chinned ostler, and then, for a moment, was alone with the dog. How much had Bunker seen? How much had he understood? Was it fancy, or did the dog crouch, the tiniest impulse, away from him as he bent to pat him? Bunker was tired; he relapsed on to his haunches, wagged his tail, grinned, but in his eyes there seemed, although the lamplight was deceptive, to be the faintest shadow of an apprehension.

"Good old dog, good old Bunker." Bunker wagged his tail, but the tiniest shiver passed, like a thought, through his body.

Olva left him.

As he passed through the streets he met men whom he knew. They nodded or flung a greeting. How strange to think that to-morrow night they would be speaking of him in low, grave voices as one who was already dead. "I knew the fellow quite well, strange, reserved man—nobody really knew him. With these foreigners, you know . . ."

Oh! he could hear them!

He passed through the gates of Saul's. The porter touched his hat. The great Centre Court was shrouded in mist, and out of the white veil the grey buildings rose, gently, on every side. There were lights now in the windows; the Chapel bell was ringing, hushed and dimmed by the heavy air. Boots rang sharply along the stone corridors. Olva crossed the court towards his room.

Suddenly, from the very heart of the mist, sharply, above the sound of the Chapel bell, a voice called—

"Carfax! Carfax!"

Olva stayed: for an instant the blood ran from his body, his knees quivered, his face was as white as the mist. Then he braced himself—he knew the voice.

"Hullo, Craven, is that you?"

"Who's that? . . . Can't see in this mist."

"Dune."

"Hullo, Dune. I say, do you know what's happened to Carfax?"

"Happened? No—why?"

"Well, I can't find him anywhere. I wanted to get him for Bridge. He ought to be back by now."

"Back? Where's he been?"

"Going over to see some aunt or other at Grantchester—ought to be back by now."

An aunt?—No, Rose Midgett.

"No—I've no idea—haven't seen him since yesterday."

"Been out for a walk?"

"Yes, just took my dog for a bit."

"See you in Hall?"

"Right—o!"

The voice began again calling under the windows—"Carfax! Carfax!"

Olva climbed the stairs to his rooms.

CHAPTER II

BUNNING

I

He went into Hall. He sat amongst the particular group of his own year who were considered the elite. There was Cardillac there, brilliant, flashing Cardillac. There was Bobby Galleon, fat, good-natured, sleepy, intelligent in an odd bovine way. There was Craven, young, ardent, hail-fellow-well-met. There was Lawrence, burly back for the University in Rugby, unintelligent, kind and good-tempered unless he were drunk.

There were others. They all sat in their glory, noisily happy. Somewhere in the distance on a raised dais were the Dons gravely pompous. Every now and again word was brought that the gentlemen were making too much noise. The Master might be observed drinking elaborately, ceremoniously with some guest. Madden, the Service Tutor, flung his shrill treble voice above the general hubbub—

"But, my dear Ross, if you had only observed—"

"Where is Carfax?" came suddenly from Lawrence. He asked Craven, who was, of course, the devoted friend of Carfax. Craven had large brown eyes, a charming smile, a prominent chin, rather fat routed cheeks and short brown hair that curled a little. He gave the impression of eager good-temper and friendliness. To-night he looked worried. "I don't know," he said, "I can't understand it. He said this morning that he'd be here to-night and make up a four at Bridge. He went off to see an aunt or some one at Grantchester!"

"Perhaps," said Bobby Galleon gravely, "he had an exeat and has gone up to town."

"But he'd have said something—sure. And the porter hasn't seen him. He would have been certain to know."

Olva was never expected to talk much. His reserve was indeed rather popular. The entirely normal and ordinary men around him appreciated this mystery. "Rum fellow, Dune . . . nobody knows him." His high dark colour, his dignity, his courtesy had about it something distinguished and romantic. "He'll do something wonderful one day, you bet. Why, if he only chose to play up at footer there's nothing he couldn't do."

Even the brilliant Cardillac, thin, dark, handsome leader of fashion and society, admitted the charm.

Now, however, Olva, looking up, quietly said—

"I expect his aunt's kept him to dinner. He'll turn up."

But of course he wouldn't turn up. He was lying in the heart of that crushed, dripping fern with his leg doubled under him. It wasn't often that one killed a man with one blow; the signet ring that he wore on the little finger of his right hand—a Dune ring of great antiquity—must have had something to do with it.

He turned it round thoughtfully on his finger. Robert, an old, old trembling waiter, said in a shaking voice—

"There's salmi of wild game, sir—roast beef."

"Beef, please," Olva said quietly.

He was considering now that all these men would to-morrow night have only one thought, one idea. They would remember everything, the very slightest thing that he had done. They would discuss it all from every possible point of view.

"I always knew he'd do something. . . ." He suddenly knew quite sharply, as though a voice had spoken to him, that he could not endure this any longer. There was gathering upon him the conviction that in a few minutes, rising from his place, he would cry out to the hall—"I, Olva Dune, this afternoon, killed Carfax. You will find his body in the wood." He repeated the words to himself under his breath. "You will find his body in the wood. . . ." "You will find . . ."

He finished his beef very quietly and then got up.

Craven appealed to him. "I say, Dune, do come and make a four—my rooms, half-past eight—Lawrence and Galleon are the other two."

Olva looked down at him with his grave, rather melancholy smile.

"Afraid I can't to-night, Craven; must work."

"Don't overdo it," Cardillac said.

The eyes of the two men met. Olva knew that Cardillac—"Cards" as he was to his friends, liked him; he himself did not hate Cardillac. He was the only man in the College for whom he had respect. They were both of them demanding the same thing from the world. They both of them despised their fellow-creatures.

Olva, climbing the stairs to his room, stood for a moment in the dark, before he turned on the lights. He spoke aloud in a whisper, as though some one were with him in the room.

"This won't do," he said. "This simply won't do. Your nerves are going. You've only got a few hours of it. Hold on—Think of the beast that he was. Think of the beast that he was."

He walked slowly back to the door and turned on the electric lights. He did not sport his oak—if people came to see him he would rather like it: in some odd way it would be more satisfactory than that he should go to see them—but people did not often come to see him.

He laid out his books on the table and sat down. He had grown fond of this room. The walls were distempered white. The ceiling was old and black with age. There was a deep red-tiled fireplace. One wall had low brown bookshelves. There were two pictures: one an Around reprint of Matsys' "Portrait of Aegidius"—that wise, kind, tender face; the other an admirable photogravure of Durer's "Selbstbildnis." The books were mainly to do with his favourite historical period—the Later Roman Empire. There was some poetry—an edition of Browning, Swinburne's Poems and Ballads, Ernest Dowson, Rossetti, Francis Thompson. There was an edition of Hazlitt, a set of the Spectator, one or two novels, Henry Lessingham and The Roads by Galleon, To Paradise by Lester, Meredith's One of Our Conquerors and Diana of the Crossways, The Ambassadors and Awkward Age of Henry James.

On the mantelpiece above the fireplace there were three deep blue bowls, the only ornaments in the room. Beyond the little diamond-paned windows, beyond the dark mysteries of the Fellows' garden, a golden mist rose from the lamps of the street, there were stars in the sky.

He faced his books. For a quarter of an hour he saw before him the hanging, baggy cheeks, the white, staring eyes, the glittering ring on the weak finger. His hands began to tremble. . . .

There was a timid knock on the door, and he was instantly sure that the body had been found, and that they had come to arrest him. He stood back from the door with his hand pressing on the table. It was almost a relief to him that the summons had come so soon—it would presently all be over.

"Come in," he said, and gave one look at the golden mist, at the stars, at the tender face of Aegidius.

The door was opened slowly with fumbling hands, and there stood there a large, fat, clumsy, shapeless creature, with a white face, a hooked nose, an open, foolish mouth.

The reaction was hysterical. To expect a summons to death and public shame, to find—Bunning. Bunning—that soft, blithering, emotional, religious, middle-class maniac—Bunning! "Soft-faced" Bunning, as he was called, was the man of Olva's year in whom the world at large found most entertainment. The son of some country clergyman, kicked and battered through the slow, dreary years at some small Public School, he had come up to Saul's with an intense, burning desire to make a mark. He was stupid, useless at games, having only somewhere behind his fat ugly body a longing to be connected with some cause, some movement, some person of whom he might make a hero.

He had, of course, within the first fortnight of his arrival, plunged himself into dire disgrace. He had asked Lawrence, coming like a young god from Marlborough, in to coffee; they had made him drunk and laughed at his hysterical tears: in his desire for popularity he had held a gathering in his room, with the original intention of coffee, cakes and gentle conversation; the evening had ended with the arrival of all his furniture and personal effects upon the grass of the court below his windows.

He had been despised by the Dons, buffeted and derided by his fellow undergraduates. Especially had Carfax and Cardillac made his life a burden to him, and whenever it seemed that there was nothing especial to do, the cry arose, "Let's go and rag Bunning," and five minutes later that fat body would tremble at the sound of many men climbing the wooden stairs, at the loud banging on his wooden door, at the cry, "Hullo, Bunning—we've come for some coffee."

Then, towards the end of the first year, the Cambridge Christian Union flung out its net and caught him. His attempt at personal popularity had failed here as thoroughly as it had failed at school—now for his soul. He found that the gentlemen of his college who were members of the Christian Union were eager for his company. They did not laugh at his conversation nor mock his proffered hospitalities. They talked to him, persuaded him that his soul was in jeopardy, and carried him off during part of the Long Vacation to the Norfolk Broads, where prayer-meetings, collisions with other sea-faring craft, and tinned meats were the order of the day.

Olva had watched him with that amused incredulity that he so frequently bestowed upon his fellow-creatures. How was this kind of animal, with its cowardice, its stupidity, its ugliness, its uselessness, possible? He had never spoken to Bunning, although he had once received a note from him asking him to coffee—a piece of very considerable impertinence. He had never assisted Carfax and Cards in their raiding expeditions, but that was only because he considered such things tiresome and childish.

And now, behold, there in his doorway—incredible vision!—was the creature—at this moment of—all others!

"Come in," said Olva again.

Bunning brought his large quivering body into the room and stood there, turning his cap round and round in his hands.

"Oh, I say—" and there he stopped.

"Won't you sit down?"

"No—thanks—I—"

"In what way can I be of use to you?"

"Oh! I say—."

Senseless giggles, and then Bunning's mouth opened and remained open. His eyes stared at Dune.

"Well, what is it?"

"Oh—my word—you know—"

"Look here," said Olva quietly, "if you don't get on and tell me what you want I shall do you some bodily damage. I've got work to do. Another time, perhaps, when I am less busy—"

Bunning was nearly in tears. "Oh, yes, I know—it's most awful cheek—I—"

There was a desperate silence and then he plunged out with—"Well, you know, I—that is—we-I—sort of wondered whether, you know, you'd care—not if you're awfully busy of course—but whether you'd care to come and hear Med. Tetloe preach to-night. I know it's most awful cheek—" He was nearly in tears.

Olva kept an amazed silence. Life! What an amusing thing!—that he, with his foot on the edge of disaster, death, should be invited by Bunning to a revival meeting. He understood it, of course. Bunning had been sent, as an ardent missionary is sent into the heart of West Africa, to invite Olva to consider his soul. He was expecting, poor creature, to be kicked violently down the twisting wooden stairs. On another occasion he would be sent to Lawrence or Cardillac, and then his expectations would be most certainly fulfilled. But it was for the cause—at least these sinners should be given the opportunity of considering their souls. If they refused to consider them, they must not complain if they find the next world but little to their fancy.

No one had ever attacked Olva before on this subject. His reserve had been more alarming to the Soul Hunters than the coarse violence of a Cardillac or a Carfax. And now Bunning—Bunning of all people in this ridiculous world—had ventured. Well, there was pluck necessary for that. Bunning, the coward, had done a braver thing than many more stalwart men would have cared to do. There was bravery there!

Moreover, why should not Olva go? He could not sit alone in his room, his nerves would soon be too many for him. What did it matter? His last evening of freedom should be spent as no other evening of his life had been spent. . . . Moreover, might there not be something behind this business? Might he not, perhaps, be shown to-night some clue to the presence of that Power that had spoken to him in the wood? Through all the tangled confusion of his thoughts, through the fear and courage there ran this note-where was God? . . . God the only person to Whom he now could speak, because God knew.

Might not this idiot of a Bunning have been shown the way to the mystery?

"Yes," said Olva, smiling. "I'll come, if you won't mind sitting down and smoking for a quarter of an hour, while I finish this—have a drink, will you?"

Bunning's consternation at Olva's acceptance was amusing. He dropped his cap, stopped to pick it up, gasped. That Dune should really come!

"You'll come?" he spluttered out. Never in his wildest imaginings had he fancied such a thing. Dune, the most secret, reserved, mysterious man in the college—Dune, whose sarcastic smile was considered more terrifying than Lawrence's mailed fist—Dune, towards whom in the back of his mind there had been paid that reverence that belongs only to those who are of another world.

Never, in anything that had happened to him, had Bunning been so terrified as he had been by this visit to Dune. Watson Morley, the Christian Union man, had insisted that it was his duty and therefore he had come, but it had taken him ten minutes of agony to climb those stairs. And now Dune had accepted. . . .

The colour flooded his cheeks and faded again. He sat down clumsily in a chair, felt for a pipe that he smoked unwillingly because it was the manly thing to do, spurted some Apollinaris into a glass and over the tablecloth, struck many matches vainly, dropped tobacco on to the carpet. His heart was beating like a hammer!

How men would stare when they saw him with Dune. In his heart was the uneasy knowledge that had Dune proposed staying there in his rooms and talking instead of going to Little St. Agnes and listening to the Reverend Med. Tetloe, he would have stayed. This was not right, it was not Christian. The world gaped below Bunning's heavy feet.

At last Dune said: "I'm ready, let's go." They went out.

II

Little St. Agnes was apparently so named because it was the largest church in Cambridge. It was of no ancient date, but it was grim, grey, dark—admirably suited to an occasion like the present. Under the high roof, lost in a grey cloud, resolving themselves into rows of white, intense faces, sat hundreds of undergraduates.

They were seated on uncomfortable, unstable chairs, and the noise of their uneasy movements sent squeaks up and down the building as though it had been a barn filled with terrified rats.

Far in the distance, perched on a high pulpit, was a little white figure—an old gaunt man with a bony hand and a grey beard. Behind him again there was darkness. Only, in all the vast place, the white body and rows of white faces raised to it.

Olva and Bunning found seats in a corner. A slight soft voice said, with the mysterious importance of one about to deliver an immense secret, "You will look in the Mission Books, Hymn 330. 'Oh! for the arms of Jesus.' I want you to think for a moment of the meaning of the words before you sing."

There followed the rustling of many pages and then a heavy, emotional silence. Olva read the words and found them very sentimental, very bad verse and rather unpleasantly fall of blood and pain. Every one stood; the chairs creaked from one end of the building to the other, an immense volume of sound rose to the roof.

Olva felt that the entire church was seized with emotion. He saw that Bunning's hand was trembling, he knew that many eyes were filled with tears. For himself, he understood at once that that distant figure in white was here to make a dramatic appeal—dramatic as certainly as the appeal that a famous actor might make in London. That was his job— he was out for it—and anything in the way of silence or noise, of darkness or light, that could add to the effect would be utilized. Olva knew also that nine-tenths of the undergraduates were present there for the same purpose. They wished to have their emotions played upon; they wished also to be reassured about life; they wished to confuse this dramatic emotion with a sincere desire for salvation. They wished, it is true, to be good, but they wished, a great deal more, to be dramatically stirred.

Olva was reminded of the tensity of the atmosphere at a bull-fight that he had once seen in Madrid. Here again was the same intensity. . . .

He saw, therefore, in this first singing of the hymn, that this place, this appeal, would be of no use in his own particular need. This deliberate evoking of dramatic effect had nothing to do with that silent consciousness of God. This place, this appeal, was fantastic, childish, beside that event that had that afternoon sent Carfax into space. Let these men hurry to the wood, let them find the sodden body, let them face then the reality of Life. . . .

Again, as before in Hall, he was tempted to rise and cry out: "I have killed Carfax. I have killed Carfax. What of all your theories now?" That trembling ass, Bunning, singing now at the top of his voice, shaking with the fervour of it, let him know that he had brought a murderer to the sacred gathering—again Olva had to concentrate all his mind, his force, his power upon the conquest of his nerves. For a moment it seemed as though he would lose all control; he stood, his knees quivering beneath him—then strength came back to him.

After the hymn the address. There was tense, rapt silence. The little voice went on, soft, low, sweet, pleading, very clear. There must be many men who had not yet found God. There were those, perhaps, in the Church tonight who had not even thought about God. There were those again who, maybe, had some crime on their conscience and did not know how to get rid of it. Would they not come to Christ and ask His help?

Stories were told. Story of the young man who cursed his mother, broke his leg, and arrived home just too late to see her alive. Story of the friend who died to save another friend, and how many souls were saved by this self-sacrifice. Story of the Undergraduate who gambled and drank and was converted by a barmaid and eventually became a Bishop.

All these examples of God's guidance. Then, for an instant, there is a great silence. The emotion is now beating in waves against the wall. The faces are whiter now, hands are clenched, lips bitten. Suddenly there leaps upon them all that gentle voice, now a trumpet. "Who is for the Lord? Who is for the Lord?"

Then gently again,—"Let us pray in silence for a few minutes." . . . A great creaking of chairs, more intense silence. At last the voice again—"Will those who are sure that they are saved stand up?" Dead silence—no one moves. "Will those who wish to be saved stand up?" With one movement every one—save only Olva, dark in his corner—stands up. Bunning's eyes are flaming, his body is trembling from head to foot.

"Christ is amongst you! Christ is in the midst of you!"

Suddenly, somewhere amongst the shadows a voice breaks out—"Oh! my God! Oh! my God!" Some one is crying—some one else is crying. All about the building men are falling on to their knees. Bunning has crashed on to his—his face buried in his hands.

The little gentle voice again—"I shall be delighted to speak to any of those whose consciences are burdened. If any who wish to see me would wait. . . ."

The souls are caught for God.

Prayers followed, another hymn. Bunning with red eyes has contemplated his sins and is in a glow of excited repentance. It is over.

As Olva rose to leave the building he knew that this was not the path for which he was searching. Not here was that terrible Presence. . . . The men poured in a black crowd out into the night. As Olva stepped into the darkness he knew that the terror was only now beginning for him. Standing there now with no sorrow, remorse, repentance, nevertheless he knew that all night, alone in his room, he would be fighting with devils. . . .

Bunning, nervously, stammered—"If you don't mind—I think I'm going round for a minute."

Olva nodded good-night. As he went on his way to Saul's, grimly, it seemed humorous that "soft-faced" Bunning should be going to confess his thin, miserable little sins.

For him, Olva Dune, only a dreadful silence. . . .

CHAPTER III

THE BODY COMES TO TOWN

I

And after all he slept, slept dreamlessly. He woke to the comfortable accustomed voices of Mrs. Ridge, his bedmaker, and Miss Annett, her assistant. It was a cold frosty morning; the sky showed through the window a cloudless blue.

He could hear the deep base voice of Mrs. Ridge in her favourite phrase: "Well, I don't think, Miss Annett. You won't get over me," and Miss Annett's mildly submissive, "I should think not indeed, Mrs. Ridge."

Lying back in bed he surveyed with a mild wonder the fact that he had thus, easily, slept. He felt, moreover, that that body had already, in the division of to-day from yesterday, lost much of its haunting power. In the clean freshness of the day, in the comfort of the casual voices of the two women in the other room, in the smell of the coffee, yesterday's melodrama seemed incredible. It had never happened; soon he would see from his window Carfax's hulking body cross the court. No, it was real enough, only it did not concern him. He watched it, as a spectator, indifferent, callous. There was a change in his life, but it was a change of another kind. In the strange consciousness that he now had of some vast and vital Presence, the temporal fact of the thing that he had done lost all importance. There was something that he had got to find, to discover. If—and the possibility seemed large now in the air of this brilliant morning—he were, after all, to escape, he would not rest until he had made his discovery. Some new life was stirring within him. He wanted now to fling himself amongst men; he would play football, he would take his place in the college, he would test everything—leave no stone unturned. No longer a cynical observer, he would be an adventurer . . . if they would let him alone.

He got out of bed, stripped, and stood over his bath. The cold air beat upon his skin; he rejoiced in the sense of his fitness, in the movement of his muscles, in the splendid condition of his body. If this were to be the last day of his freedom, it should at any rate be a splendid day.

He had his bath, flung on a shirt and trousers and went into his sitting-room, bright now with the morning sun, so that the blue bowls and the red tiles shone, and even the dark face of Aegidius was lighted with the gleam.

Mrs. Ridge was short and stout, with white hair, a black bonnet, and the deepest of voices. Her eagerness to deliver herself of all the things that she wanted to say prevented full-stops and commas from being of any use to her. Miss Annett was admirably suited as a companion, being long, thin and silent, and intended by nature to be subservient to the more masterful of her sex. With any man she was able easily to hold her own; with Mrs. Ridge she was bending, bowed, humility.

Mrs. Ridge grinned like a dog at the appearance of Olva. "Good mornin', sir, and a nice frosty cold sort o' day it is with Miss Annett just breakin' one of your cups, sir, 'er 'ands bein' that cold and a cup bein' an easy thing to slip out of the 'and as you must admit yourself, sir. Pore Miss Annett is that distressed."

Miss Annett did indeed look downcast. "I can't think—" she began.

"It's quite all right, Miss Annett," said Olva. "I think it's wonderful that you break the things as seldom as you do. The china was of no kind of value."

It was known in the college that Mr. Dune was the only gentleman of whom Mrs. Ridge could be said to be afraid; she was proud of him and frightened of him. She said to Miss Annett, when that lady made her first appearance—

"And I can tell you, Miss Annett, that you need never 'ave no fear of bein' introjuced to Royalty one of these days after bein' with that Mr. Dune, because it puts you in practice, I can tell you, and a nice spoken gentleman 'e is and quiet—never does a thing 'e shouldn't, but wicked under it all I'll be bound. 'E's no chicken, you take it from me. Born yesterday? I don't think. . . ."

The women faded away, and he was left to himself. After breakfast he thought that he would write to his father and give him an account of the thing that he had done; if he escaped suspicion he would tear it up. Also he was determined on two things: one was that if he were accused of the crime, he would at once admit everything; the other was that he would do his utmost, until he was accused, to lead his life exactly as though he were in no way concerned. He had now an odd assurance that it was not by his public condemnation that he was intended to work out the results of his act. Why was he so assured of that? What was it that was now so strangely moving him? He faced the world, armed, resolved. It seemed to him that it was important for him, now, to live. This was the first moment of his life that existence had appeared to be of any moment. He wanted time to continue his search.

He wrote to his father—

MY DEAR FATHER,—

I have just been arrested on the charge of murdering an undergraduate here called Carfax. It is quite true that I killed him. We met yesterday, in the country, quarrelled, and I struck him, hitting him on the chin. He fell instantly, breaking his neck. He was muck of the worst kind. I had known him at Rugby; he was always a beast of the lowest order. He was ruining a fellow here, taking his money, making him drink, doing for him; also ruining a girl in a tobacconist's shop. All this was no business of mine, but we had always loathed one another. I think when I hit him I wanted to kill him. I am not, in any way, sorry, except that suddenly I do not want to die. You are the only person in the world for whom I care; you will understand. I have not disgraced the name; it was killing a rat. I think that you had better not come to see me. I face it better alone. We have gone along well together, you and I. I send you my love. Good-bye, OLVA.

As he finished it, he wondered, Would this be sent? Would they come for him? Perhaps, at this moment, they had found the body. He put the letter carefully in the pocket of his shirt. Then, suddenly, he was confronted with the risk. Suppose that he were to be taken ill, to faint, to forget the thing. . . . No, the letter must wait. They would allow him to write, if the time came.

He took the letter, flung it into the fire, watched it burn. He felt as though, in the writing of it, he had communicated with his father. The old man would understand.

II

About eleven o'clock Craven came to see him. Craven's father had been a Fellow of Trinity and Professor of Chinese to the University. He had died some five years ago and now the widow and young Craven's sister lived in Cambridge. Craven had tried, during his first term, to make a friend of Olva, but his happy, eager attitude to the whole world had seemed crude and even priggish to Olva's reserve, and all Craven's overtures had been refused, quietly, kindly, but firmly. Craven had not resented the repulse; it was not his habit to resent anything, and as the year had passed, Olva had realized that Craven's impetuous desire for the friendship of the world was something in him perfectly natural and unforced. Olva had discovered also that Craven's devotion to his mother and sister was the boy's leading motive in life. Olva had only seen the girl, Margaret, once; she had been finishing her education in Dresden, and he remembered her as dark, reserved, aloof—opposite indeed from her brother's cheerful good-fellowship. But for Rupert Craven this girl was his world; she was obviously cleverer, more temperamental than he, and he felt this and bowed to it.

These things Olva liked in him, and had the boy not been so intimate with Cardillac and Carfax, Olva might have made advances, Craven took a man of the Carfax type with extreme simplicity; he thought his geniality and physical strength excused much coarseness and vulgarity. He was still young enough to have the Public School code—the most amazing thing in the history of the British nation—and because Carfax bruised his way as a forward through many football matches, and fought a policeman on Parker's Piece one summer evening, Rupert Craven thought him a jolly good fellow. Carfax also had had probably, at the bottom of his dirty, ignoble soul, more honest affection for Craven than for any one in the world. He had tried to behave himself in that ingenuous youth's company.

Now young Craven, disturbed, unhappy, anxious, stood in Olva's door.

"I say, Dune, I hope I'm not disturbing you?"

"Not a bit."

"It's a rotten time to come." Craven came in and sat down. "I'm awfully worried."

"Worried?"

"Yes, about Carfax. No one knows what's happened to him. He may have gone up to town, of course, but if he did he went without an exeat. Thompson saw him go out about two-thirty yesterday afternoon—was going to Grantchester, because he yelled it back to Cards, who asked him where he was off to—not been heard or seen since."

"Oh, he's sure to be all right," Olva said easily.

"He's up in town!"

"Yes, I expect he is, but I don't know that that makes it any better. There's some woman he's been getting in a mess with I know—didn't say anything to me about it, but I heard of it from Cards."

"Well—" Olva slowly lit his pipe—"there's something else too. He was always in with a lot of these roughs in the town—stable men and the rest. He used to get tips from them, he always said, and he's had awful rows with some of them before now. You know what a temper he's got, especially when he's been drinking at all. I shouldn't wonder if he hadn't a fight one fine day and got landed on the chin, or something, and left."

"Oh! Carfax can look after himself all right. He's used to that kind of company."

Olva gazed, through the smoke of his pipe, dreamily into the fire.

"You don't like him," Craven said suddenly.

Olva turned slowly in his chair and looked at him. "Why! What makes you say that?"

"Something Carfax told me the other day. We were sitting one evening in his room and he suddenly said to me, 'You know there is one fellow in this place who hates me like poison—always has hated me.' I asked him who it was. He said it was you. I was immensely surprised, because I'd always thought you very good friends—as good friends as you ever are with any one, Dune. You don't exactly take any of us to your breast, you know!"

Dune smiled. "No, I think I've made a mistake in keeping so much alone. It looks as though I thought myself so damned superior. But I assure you Carfax was—is—quite wrong. We've been friendly enough all our days."

"No," said Craven slowly, "I don't think you do like him. I've watched you since. He's an awfully good fellow—really—at heart, you know. I do hope things are all right. I sent off a wire to his uncle in town half an hour ago to ask whether he were there. I don't know why I'm so anxious. . . . It's all right, of course, but I'm uneasy."

"Well, you're quite wrong about my disliking Carfax," Olva went on. "And I think, altogether, it's about time I came off my perch. For one thing I'm going to take up Rugger properly."

"Oh, but that's splendid! Will you play against St. Martin's to-morrow? It will relieve Lawrence like anything if you will. They've got Cards, Worcester and Tundril, and they want a fourth Three badly. My word, Dune, that would be splendid. We'll have you a Blue after all."

"A little late for that, I'm afraid."

"Not a bit of it. They keep on changing the Threes. Of course Cards is having a good shot at it, but he isn't down against the Harlequins on Saturday, and mighty sick he is about it." Craven got up to go. "Well, I must be moving. Perhaps Carfax is back in his rooms. There may be word of him anyway."

Olva's pipe was out. The matchbox on the mantelpiece was empty. He felt in his pocket for the little silver box that he always carried. It was a box, with the Dune arms stamped upon it, that his father had given to him. He had it, he remembered, yesterday when he set out on his walk. He felt in all his pockets. These were the clothes that he was wearing yesterday. Perhaps it was in his bedroom. He went in to look, and Craven meanwhile watched him from the door.

"What have you lost?"

"Nothing."

It was not in the bedroom. He felt in the overcoat that he had been wearing. It was not there.

"Nothing. It's a matchbox of mine—must have dropped out of a pocket."

"Sorry. Daresay it will turn up. Well, see you later."

Craven vanished; then suddenly put his head in through the door.

"Oh, I say, Dune, come in to supper to-morrow night. Home I mean. My sister's back from Dresden, and I'd like you to know her. I'm sure you'd get on."

"Thanks very much, I'd like to come." Olva stood in the centre of the room, his hands clenched, his face white. He must have dropped the box in the wood. He had it on his walk, he had lit his pipe. . . . Of course they would find it. Here then was the end. Now for the first time the horror of death came upon him, filing the room, turning it black, killing the fire, the colour. His body was frozen with horror— already his throat was choking, his eyes burning. The room swung slowly round him, turning, turning. "They shan't take me. . . . They shan't take me." His face was cruel, his mouth twisted. He saw the little silver box lying there, open, exposed, upon the grass, glittering against the dull green. He turned to the window with desperate, hunted eyes. Already he fancied that he heard their steps upon the stair. He stood, his body flung back, his hands pressing upon the table. "They shan't take me. . . . They shan't take me." The door turned, slowly opened. It was Mrs. Ridge with a duster. He gave a little sigh and rolled over, tumbling back against the chair, unconscious.

III

"There, sir, now I do 'ope as you'll be all right. Too much book-work, that's what it is, but if a doctor—"

Olva was lying in his chair now, very pale, his eyes closed.

"No, thank you, Mrs. Ridge. It's all right now, thank you—quite all right. Yes, I'm ready for lunch—very silly of me."

Mrs. Ridge departed to fetch the luncheon-dish from the College kitchens and to tell the porter Thompson all about it on the way. "Pore young gentleman, there 'e was as you might say white as a sheet all of a 'eap. It gave me a turn I can assure you, Mr. Thompson."

His lunch was untasted. It seemed to him that he had now lost all power of control. He could only face the inevitable fact of his approaching capture. The sudden discovery of the loss of the matchbox had clanged the facts about his ears with the discordant scream of closing gates. He was captured, caught irretrievably, like a rat in a trap. He did not wish to be caught like a rat in a trap. This was a free world. Air, light, colour were about him on every side. To die, fighting, on a hill-top, in a battle-field, that was one thing. To see them crowding into his room, to be dragged into a dark airless place, to be caught by the neck and throttled. . . .

Mrs. Ridge cleared away the lunch with much shaking of the head. Olva lay in his chair watching, with eyes that never closed nor stirred, the crackling golden fire. Beyond the window the world was of blue steel. He could fancy the still gleaming waters of the lake that stretched beyond the grass lawns; he could fancy the red brick of the buildings that clung like some frieze to the horizon. Along the stone courtyard rang the heavy football boots of men going to the Upper Fields. He could see their red and blue jerseys, their short blue trousers, their tight stockings—the healthy swing of their bodies as they tramped. Men would be going down to the river now—freshmen would be hearing reluctantly, some of them with tears, the coarse and violent criticism of the Third Year men who were tabbing them. All the world was moving. He was surrounded, there in his silent room, with an amazing sense of life. He seemed to realize, for the first time, what it was that Cambridge was doing . . . all this physical life marching through the cold bright air, strength, poetry, the great stir and enthusiasm of the Young Blood of the world . . . and he, waiting for those steps on the stair, for those grim faces in the open door. The world left him alone. As the afternoon advanced, the tramp of the footballers was no longer heard, silence, bound by the shining frost of the beautiful day, lay about the grey buildings. Soon a melody of thrumming kettles would rise into the air, in every glowing room tea would be preparing, the glorious luxury of rest after stinging exercise would fill the courts with worship, unconsciously driven, skywards, to the Powers of Health. And then, after years of time, as it seemed, faintly through the closed windows at last came the single note of St. Martin's bell. That meant that it was quarter to five. Almost unconsciously he rose, put on his cap and gown and passed through the twilit streets that were stealing now into a dim glow under their misty lamps. The great chapel of St. Martin's, planted like some couchant animal grey and mysterious against the blue of the evening sky, flung through its windows the light of its many candles. He found a seat at the back of the dark high-hanging ante-chapel. He was alone there. Towards the inner chapel the white-robed choir moved softly; for a moment the curtains were drawn aside revealing the misty candle-light within; the white choir passed through—the curtains Fell again, leaving Olva alone with the great golden trumpeting angels above the organ for his company.

Then great peace came upon him. Some one had taken his soul, softly, with gentle hands, and was caring for it. He was suddenly freed from responsibility, and as the soothing comfort stole about him he knew that now he had simply to wait to be shown what it was that he must do. This was not the strange indifference of yesterday, nor the physical strength of the morning . . . peace, such peace as he had never before known, had come to him. From the heart of the darkness up into the glowing beauty of the high roof the music rose. It was Wednesday afternoon and the voices were un accompanied. Soon the Insanae et Vanae climbed in wave after wave of melody, was caught, held, lingered in the air, softly died again.

Olva was detached—he saw his body beaten, imprisoned, tortured, killed. But he was not there. He was riding heaven in quest of God.

IV

At the gates of his college the news met him. He had been waiting for it so long a time that now he had to act his horror. It seemed to him an old, old story—this tale of a murder in Sannet Wood.

Groups of men were waiting in the cloisters, waiting for the doors to open for "Hall." As Olva came towards the gates an undergraduate, white, breathless, brushed past him and burst into the quiet, murmuring groups.

"My God, have you heard?"

Olva passed through the iron gates. The groups broke. He had the impression of many men standing back—black in the dim light—waiting, listening.

There was an instant's silence. Then, the man's voice breaking into a shrill scream, the news came tumbling out. It seemed to flash a sudden glare upon the blackness.

"It's Carfax—Carfax—he's been murdered."

The word was tossed, caught, flung against the stone pillars— "Murdered! Murdered! Murdered!"

"They've just brought his body in now, found it in Sannet Wood this evening; a working man found it. Been there two days. His neck broken—"

The mysterious groups scattered into strange fantastic shapes. There was a pause and then a hundred voices began at once. Some one spoke to Olva and he answered; his voice low and stern. . . . On every side confusion.

But for himself, like steel armour encasing his body, was the strange calm—aloof, unmoved, dispassionate—that had come to him half an hour ago.

He was alone—like God.

CHAPTER IV

MARGARET CRAVEN

I

It is essential to the maintenance of the Cambridge spirit that there should be no melodrama. Into that placid and speculative air real life tumbles with a resounding shock and the many souls that have been building, these many years, with careful elaboration, walls of defence and protection find themselves suddenly naked and indecent before the world. For that army of men who use Cambridge as a gate to the world in front of them the passage through the narrow streets is too swift to afford more in after life than a pleasant reminiscence. It is because Cambridge is the bridge between stern discipline and pleasant freedom that it is so happily remembered; but there are those who adopt Cambridge as their abiding home, and it is for these that real life is impossible.

Beneath these grey walls as the years pass slowly the illusions grow. Closer and closer creep the walls of experience, softer and thicker are the garments worn to keep out the cold, gentler and gentler are the speculations born of a good old Port and a knowledge of the Greek language. About the High Tables voices softly dispute the turning of a phrase, eyes mildly salute the careful dishes of a wisely chosen cook, gentle patronage is bestowed upon the wild ruffian of the outer world. Many bells ring, many fires are burning, many lamps are lit, many leaves of many books are turned—busily, busily hands are raising walls of self-defence; the world at first regretted, then patronized, is now forgotten . . . hush, he sleeps, his feet in slippers, his head upon the softest cushion, his hand still covering the broad page of his dictionary. . . . Nothing, not birth nor love, nor death must disturb his repose.

And here, in the heart of the Sannet Wood, is death from violence, death, naked, crude, removed from all sense of life as we know it. The High Tables avoid Carfax's body with all possible discretion; for an hour or two the Port has lost its flavour, Homer is hidden by a cloud, the gentle chatter is curtailed and silenced. Amongst the lower order—those wild and turbulent undergraduates—it is the only topic. Carfax is very generally known; he had ridden, he had rowed, he had played cricket. A member of the only sporting club in the University, he had been known as a "real sportsman and a damned good fellow" because he was often drunk and frequently spent an evening in London . . . and now he is dead.

In Saul's a number of very young spirits awake to the consciousness of death. Here is a red-faced hearty fellow as fit as anything one moment and dead the next. Never before had the fact been faced that this might happen to any one. Let the High Table dismiss it easily, it is none so simple for those who have not had time to build up those defending walls. For a day or two there is a hush about the place, voices are soft, men talk in groups, the mystery is the one sensation. . . . The time passes, there are other interests, once more the High Table can taste its wine. Death is again bundled into noisier streets, into a harder, shriller air. . . .

II

Olva, on the morning after the discovery of the body, heard from Mrs. Ridge speculations as to the probable criminal. "You take my word, Mr. Dune, sir, it was one of them there nasty tramps—always 'anging round they are, and Miss Annett was only yesterday speakin' to me of a ugly feller comin' round to their back door and askin' for bread, weren't you, Miss Annett?"

"I was, indeed, Mrs. Ridge."

"And 'im with the nastiest 'eavy blue jaw you ever saw on a man, 'adn't 'e, Miss Annett?"

"He had, indeed, Mrs. Ridge."

"Ah, I shouldn't wonder—nasty-sort-o'-looking feller. And that Sannet Wood too—nasty lonely place with its old stones and all—comfortable?—I don't think."

Olva made inquiries as to the stones.

"Why, ever so old, they say—before Christ, I've 'eard. Used to cut up 'uman flesh and eat it like the pore natives, and there's a ugly lookin' stone in that very wood where they did it too, or so I've 'eard. Would you go along that way in the dark, Miss Annett?"

"Not much—I grant you, Mrs. Ridge."

"Oh yes! not likely on a dark night, I don't think!—and that pore Mr. Carfax—well, all I say is, I 'opes they catch 'im, that's all I say . . ." with further reminiscence concerning Mrs. Birch who had worked on Carfax's staircase the last ten years and never "'ad no kind of luck. There was that Mr. Oliver—"

Final dismissal of Mrs. Ridge and Miss Annett.

Meanwhile, strange enough the relief that he felt because the body was actually removed from that wood. No longer possible now to see it lying there with the leg bent underneath, the head falling straight back, the ring on the finger. . . . Curious, too, that the matchbox had not been discovered; they must have searched pretty thoroughly by now—perhaps after all it had not been dropped there.

But over him there had fallen a strange lassitude. He was outside, beyond it all.

And then Craven came to see him. The event had wrought in the boy a great change. It was precisely with a character like Craven's that such an incident must cleave a division between youth and manhood. He had, until last evening, considered nothing for himself; his father's death had occurred when he was too young to see anything in it but a perfectly natural removal of some one immensely old. The world had seemed the easiest, the simplest of places, his years at Rugby had been delight. Fully free from shocks of any kind. Good health, friendship, a little learning, these things had made the days pass swiftly. Rupert Craven had been yesterday, a child precisely typical of the system in which he had been drilled; now he was something different. Olva knew that he was capable of depths of feeling because of his extraordinary devotion to his sister. Craven had often spoken of her to Olva—"So different from me, the most brilliant person in the world. Her music is really wonderful—people who know, I mean, all say so. But you see we're the same age—only two of us. We've always been everything to one another."

Olva wondered why Craven had told him. It was not as though they had ever been very intimate, but Craven seemed to think that Olva and his sister would have much in common.

Olva wondered, as he looked at Craven standing there in the doorway, how this sister would take the change in her brother. He had suddenly, as he looked at Craven, a perception of the number of lives with whose course his action had involved him. The wheel was beginning to turn. . . .

The light had gone from Craven's eyes. His vitality and energy had slipped from him, leaving his body heavy, unalert. He seemed puzzled, awed; there were dark lines under his eyes, his cheeks were pale and his mouth had lost its tendency to smile, its lines were heavy; but, above all, his expression was interrogative. Finally, he was puzzled.

For an instant, as he looked at him, Olva felt that he could not face him, then with a deliberate summoning of the resources of his temperament he strung himself to whatever the day might bring forth.

"This is awful—"

"Yes."

"Of course it doesn't matter to you, Dune, as it does to me, but I knew the fellow so awfully well. It's horrible, horrible. That he should have died—like that."

Olva broke out suddenly. "After all not such a bad way to die—swift enough. I don't suppose Carfax valued life especially."

"Oh! he enjoyed it—enjoyed it like anything. And that it should be taken so trivially, for no reason at all. It seems to be almost certain that it was some tramp or other—robbery the motive probably, and then he was startled and left the money—it was all lying about on the grass. But then Carfax was mixed up with so many ruffians of one kind and another. It may have been revenge or any-thing. I believe they are searching the wood now, but they're not likely to bring it home to any one. Misty day, no one about, and the man simply used his fist apparently—he must have been most awfully strong. Have you ever heard of any one killing a man with one blow—except a prize-fighter?"

"It's simply a knack, I believe, if you catch a fellow in a certain spot."

Supposing that some wretched tramp were arrested and accused? Some dirty fellow from behind a hedge? All the tramps, all the ruffians of the world were now a danger. The accusation of another would bring the truth from him of course. His dark eyes moved across the room to Craven's white, tired face. Within himself there moved now with every hour stirring more acutely this desire for life. If only they would let him alone . . . let the body alone . . . let it all alone. Let the world sink back to its earlier apathy.

His voice was resentful.

"Carfax wasn't a good fellow, Craven. No, I know—Nil nini bonum . . . and all the rest of it. But it looks a bit like a judgment—judgment from Heaven."

Craven broke in.

"But now—just now when his body's lying there. I know there were things he did. He was a bit wild, of course—"

"Yes, there was a girl, a girl in Midgett's tobacconist's shop—his daughter. Carfax ruined her, body and soul . . . ruined her. He boasted of it. Looks like a judgment."

"I don't care." Craven sprang up. "Carfax may have done things, but he was a friend of mine, and a good friend. They must catch the man, they must. It's a duty they owe us all. To have such a man as that hanging about. Why, it might happen to any of us. You must help me, Dune."

"Help you?"

"Yes—help them to catch the murderer. We must think of everything that could make a clue. Perhaps this girl. I had heard something about her, of course; but perhaps there was another lover, a rival or something, or perhaps her father—"

"Well," Dune said slowly, "my advice to you, Craven, is not to think too much about the whole business. A thing like that is certain to get on one's nerves—leave it alone as much as you can—"

"What a funny chap you are! You're always like that. As detached from everything as though you weren't alive at all. Why, I believe, if you'd committed the murder yourself you wouldn't be much more concerned!"

"Well, we've got to go on as we're made, I suppose, only do take my advice about not getting morbid over it. By the way, I see I'm playing against St. Martin's this afternoon."

"Yes. I thought at first I wouldn't play. But I suppose it's better to go on doing one's ordinary things. You're coming in to-night, aren't you?"

"Are you sure you want me after all this disturbance?"

"Why, of course; my mother's expecting you. Half-past seven. Don't dress." He raised his arms above his head, yawning. He was obviously better for the talk. His eyes were less strained, his body more alert. "I'm tired to death. Didn't get a wink of sleep last night—saw poor Carfax in the dark—ugh! Well, we meet this afternoon."

When the door closed Olva had the sensation of having been on his trial. Craven's eyes still followed him. Nerves, of course . . . but they had strangely reminded him of Bunker.

III

Olva had never been to Craven's house before. It stood in a little street that joined Cambridge to the country. At one end of the prim little road the lamps stopped abruptly and a white chalk path ran amongst dark common to a distant wood.

At the other end a broader road with tram-lines crossed. The house was built by itself, back from the highway, with a tiny drive and some dark laurels. It was always gloomy and apparently unkept. The autumn leaves were dull and sodden upon the drive; the bell and knocker upon the heavy door, from which the paint was worn in places, were rusty. No sound came from the little road beyond.

The place seemed absolutely without life. Olva now, as he sent the bell pealing through the passages, knew that this dark desertion had an effect upon his nerves. A week ago he would not have noticed the place at all—now he longed for lights and noise and company. He had played foot-ball that afternoon better than ever before; that, too, had been a defence, almost a protest, an assertion of his right to live.

As he waited his thoughts pursued him. He had heard them say to-night that no clue had been discovered, that the police were entirely at a loss. It was impossible to trace foot-marks amongst all that undergrowth. No one had been seen in that direction during the hours when the murder must have been committed . . . so on—so on . . . all this talk, this discussion. The wretched man was dead—no one would miss him—no one cared—leave him alone, leave him alone. Olva pulled the bell again furiously. Why couldn't they come? He wanted to escape from this dark and dismal drive; these hanging laurels, the cold little road, with its chilly lamps. An old and tottering woman, her nose nearly touching her chin and her fingers in black mittens, opened at last and led Olva into the very blackest and closest little hall that he had ever encountered. The air was thick and musty with a strangely mingled smell of burning wood, of faded pot-pourri, of dried skins. The ceiling was low and black, and the only window was one of a dull red glass that glimmered mournfully at a distance. The walls were hung with the strangest things, prizes apparently that the late Dr. Craven had secured in China—grinning heathen gods, uncouth weapons, dried skins of animals. Out of this dark little hall Olva was led into a drawing-room that was itself nearly as obscure. Here the ceiling was higher, but the place square and dark; a deep set stone fireplace in which logs were burning was the most obvious thing there. For the rest the floor seemed littered with old twisted tables, odd chairs with carved legs, here a plate with sea shells, here a glass case with some pieces of ribbon, old rusty coins, silver ornaments. There were many old prints upon the walls, landscapes, some portraits, and stuck here and there elaborate arrangements of silk and ribbon and paper fans and coloured patterns. Opposite the dark diamond-paned window was an old gilt mirror that seemed to catch all the room into its dusty and faded reflections, and to make what was old and tattered enough already, doubly dreary. The room had the close and musty air of the hall as though windows were but seldom opened; there was a scent as though oranges had recently been eaten there.

At first Olva had thought that he was alone in the room; then when his eyes had grown more accustomed to the light he saw, sitting in a high-backed chair, motionless, gazing into the fire, with her fine white hands lying in her lap, a lady. She reminded him, in that first vision of her, of "Phiz's" pictures of Mrs. Clennam in Little Dorrit, and always afterwards that connection remained with him. Her thin, spare figure had something intense, almost burning, in its immobility, in the deep black of her dress and hair, in the white sharpness of the outline of her face.

How admirably, it seemed to him, she suited that room. She too may have thought as she turned slowly to look at him that he fitted his background, with the spare dignity of his figure, his fine eyes, the black and white contrast of his body so that his cheeks, his hands, seemed almost to shine against the faded air. It is certain that they recognized at once some common ground so that they met as though they had known one another for many years. The old minor caught for a moment the fine gravity and silence of his approach to her as he waited for her to greet him.

But before she could speak to him the door had opened and Margaret Craven entered. In her gravity, her silence, she seemed at once to claim kinship with them both. She had the black hair, the pale face, the sharp outline of her mother. As she came quietly towards them her reserve was wonderful, but there was tenderness in the soft colour of her eyes, in the lines of her mouth that made her also beautiful. But beyond the tenderness there was also an energy that made every move seem like an attack. In spite of her reserve there was impatience, and Olva's first judgment of her was that the last thing in the world that she could endure was muddle; she shone with the clean-cut decision of fine steel.

Mrs. Craven spoke without rising from her chair.

"I am very glad to see you, Mr. Dune, Rupert has often told us about you."

Margaret advanced to him and held out her hand. She looked him straight in the eyes.

"We have met before, you know."

"I had not forgotten," he answered her gravely.

Then Rupert came in. It was strange how one saw now, when he stood beside his mother and sister, that he had some of their quality of stern reserve. He had always seemed to Olva a perfectly ordinary person of natural good health and good temper, and now this quality that had descended upon him increased the fresh attention that he had already during these last two days demanded. For something beyond question the Carfax affair must be held responsible. It seemed now to be the only thing that could hold his mind. He spoke very little, but his white face, his tired eyes, his listless conversation, showed the occupation of his mind. It was indeed a melancholy evening.

To Olva, his nerves being already on edge, it was almost intolerable. They passed from the drawing-room into a tiny dining-room—a room that was as dingy and faded as the rest, with a dull red paper on the walls and an old blue carpet. The old woman waited; the food was of the simplest.

Mrs. Craven scarcely spoke at all. She sat with her eyes gravely fixed in front of her, save when she raised them to flash them for an instant at Olva. He found this sudden gaze extraordinarily disconcerting; it was as though she were reasserting her claim to some common understanding that existed between them, to some secret that belonged to them alone.

They avoided, for the most part, Carfax's death. Once Margaret Craven said: "One of the most astonishing things about anything of this kind seems to me the bravery of the murderer—the bravery I mean that is demanded of any one during the days between the crime and his arrest. To be in possession of that tremendous secret, to be at war, as it were, with the world, and yet to lead, in all probability, an ordinary life—that demands courage."

"One may accustom oneself to anything," Mrs. Craven said. Her voice was deep and musical, and her words seemed to linger almost like an echo in the air.

Olva thought as he looked at Margaret Craven that there was a strength there that could face anything; it was more than courage; it might, under certain circumstances, become fanaticism. But he knew that whereas Mrs. Craven stirred in him a deep restlessness and disquiet, Margaret Craven quieted and soothed him, almost, it seemed, deliberately, as though she knew that he was in trouble.

He said: "I should think that his worst enemy, if he have any imagination at all, must be his loneliness. I can conceive that the burden of the secret, even though there be no chance whatever of discovery, must make that loneliness intolerable."

Here Rupert Craven interrupted as though he were longing to break away from the subject.

"You played the finest game of your life this afternoon, Dune. I never saw anything like that last try of yours. Whymper was on the touch-line—I saw him. The 'Varsity's certain to try you again on Saturday."

"I've been slack too long," Olva said, laughing. "I never enjoyed anything more than this afternoon."

"I played the most miserable game I've ever played—couldn't get this beastly thing out of my head."

Olva felt as though he were almost at the end of his endurance. At that moment he thought that he would have preferred them to burst the doors and arrest him. He had never known such fatigue. If he could sleep he did not care what happened to him.

The rest of the evening seemed a dream. The dark, crowded drawing-room flickered in the light from the crackling fire. Mrs. Craven, in her stiff chair, never moving her eyes, flung shadows on the walls. Some curtain blew drearily, with little secret taps, against the door. Rupert Craven sat moodily in a dark corner.

At Olva's request Margaret Craven played. The piano was old and needed attention, but he thought that he had never heard finer playing. First she gave him some modern things—some Debussy, Les Miroires of Ravel, some of the Russian ballet music of Cleopatre. These she flung at him, fiercely, aggressively, playing them as though she would wring cries of protest from the very notes.

"There," she cried when she had finished, flashing a look that was almost indignant at him. "There is your modern stuff—I can give you more of it."

"I would like something better now," he said gravely.

Without a word that mood left her. In the dim candle-light her eyes were tender again. Very softly she played the first two movements of the "Moonlight" sonata.

"I am not in the mood for the last movement," she said, and closed the piano. Still about the old silver, the dark walls, the log fire, the old gilt mirror, the sweet, delicate notes lingered.

Soon afterwards he left them. As he passed down the chill, deserted street, abandoning the dark laurelled garden, he saw behind him the stern shadow of Mrs. Craven black upon the wall.

But the loneliness, the unrest, walked behind him. Silence was beginning to be terrible. God—this God—this Unknown God—pursued him. Only a little comfort out of the very heart of that great pursuing shadow came to him—Margaret Craven's grave and tender eyes.

CHAPTER V

STONE ALTARS

I

Carfax was buried. There had been an inquest; certain tramps and wanderers had been arrested, examined and dismissed. No discovery had been made, and a verdict of Wilful "Wilful murder against some person or persons unknown" had been returned. It was generally felt that Carfax's life had not been of the most savoury and that there were, in all probability, amongst the back streets of Cambridge several persons who had owed him a grudge. He appeared, indeed, in the discoveries that were now made on every side, to be something better dead than alive. A stout and somnolent gentleman, with red cheeks and eyes half closed, was the only mourner from the outside world at the funeral. This, it appeared, was an uncle. Father dead, mother divorced and leading a pleasant existence amongst the capitals of Europe. The uncle, although maintaining a decent appearance of grief, was obviously, at heart, relieved to be rid of his nephew so easily. Poor Carfax! For so rubicund and noisy a person he left strangely little mark upon the world. Within a fortnight the college had nearly lost account of his existence. He lent to Sannet Wood a sinister air that caused numberless undergraduates to cycle out in that direction. Now and again, when conversation flagged, some one revived the subject. But it was a horse that needed much whipping to make it go. It had kicked with its violent hoof upon the soft walls of Cambridge life. For a moment it had seemed that it would force its way, but the impression had been of the slightest.

Even within the gates and courts of Saul's itself the impression that Carfax had left faded with surprising swiftness into a melodramatic memory. But nothing could have been more remarkable than the resolute determination of these young men to push grim facts away. They were not made—one could hear it so eloquently explained—for that kind of tragedy. The autumn air, the furious exercise, the hissing kettles, the decent and amiable discussions on Life reduced to the importance of a Greek Accent—these things rejected violently the absurdity of Tragic Crudity.

They were quite right, these young men. They paid their shining pounds for the capture—conscious or not as it might be—of an atmosphere, a delicate and gentle setting to the crudity of their later life. Carfax, when alive, had blundered into coarse disaster but had blundered in back streets. Now the manner of his death painted him in shrieking colours. The harmony was disturbed, therefore he must go.

Of more importance to this world of Saul's was the strange revival—as though from the dead—of Olva Dune. They had been prepared, many of them, for some odd development, but this perfectly normal, healthy interest in the affairs of the College was the last thing that his grave, romantic air could ever have led any one to expect. His football in the first place opened wide avenues of speculation. First there had been the College game, then there had been the University match against the Harlequins, and it was, admittedly, a very long time since any one had seen anything like it. He had seemed, in that game against the Harlequins, to possess every virtue that should belong to the ideal three-quarter—pace, swerve, tackle, and through them all the steady working of the brain. Nevertheless those earlier games were yet remembered against him, and it was confidently said that this brilliance, with a man of Dune's temperament, could not possibly last. But, nevertheless, the expectation of his success brought him up, with precipitation, against the personality of Cardillac, and it was this implied rivalry that agitated the College. It is only in one's second year that a matter of this kind can assume world-shaking importance.

The First-year Undergraduate is too near the child, the Third-year Undergraduate too near the man. For the First-year man School, for the Third-year man the World looms too heavily. So it is from the men of the Second year that the leaders are to be selected, and at this time in Saul's Cardillac seemed to have no rival. He combined, to an admirable degree, the man of the world and the sportsman; he had an air that was beyond rubies. He was elegant without being effeminate, arrogant without being conceited, indifferent without being blase. He had learnt, at Eton, and at the knee of a rich and charming mother, that to be crude was the unforgivable sin. He worshipped the god of good manners and would have made an admirable son of the great Lord Chesterfield. Finally he was the only man in Saul's who had any "air" at all, and he had already travelled round the world and been introduced by his mother to Royalty at Marienbad.

The only man who could ever have claimed any possible rivalry was Dune, and Dune had seemed determined, until now, to avoid any-thing of the kind. Suddenly the situation leapt upon the startled eyes of the attentive world. Possibility of excitement. . . .

II

Olva, himself, was entirely unconcerned by this threatened rivalry. He was being driven, by impulses that he understood only too well, into the noisiest life that he could manage to find about him. The more noise the better; he had only a cold fear at his heart that, after all, it would penetrate his dreaded loneliness too little, let it be as loud a noise as he could possibly summon.

He had not now—and this was the more terrible—any consciousness of Carfax at all; there was waiting for him, lurking, beast-like, until its inevitable moment, something far more terrible.

Meanwhile he made encounters. . . . There was Bunning. The Historical Society in Saul's was held together by the Senior Tutor. This gentleman, a Mr. Gregg, was thin, cadaverous, blue-chinned, mildly insincere. It was his view of University life that undergraduates were born yesterday and would believe anything that you told them. In spite, however, of their tender years there was a lurking ferocity that must be checked by an indulgent heartiness of manner, as one might offer a nut to a monkey. His invariable manner of salutation—"Come along, Simter—the very man I wanted to see"—lost its attraction through much repetition, and the hearty assumption on the amiable gentleman's part that "we are all boys together" froze many undergraduates into a chill and indifferent silence. He had not taken Holy Orders, but he gave, nevertheless, the effect of adopting the language of the World, the Flesh and the Devil in order that he might the better spy out the land. He attracted, finally, to himself certain timid souls who preferred insincere comfort to none at all, but he was hotly rejected by more able-bodied persons.

Nevertheless the Historical Society prospered, and Olva one evening, driven he knew not by what impulse, attended its meeting. When he entered Mr. Gregg's room some dozen men were already seated there. The walls were hung with groups in which a younger and even thinner Mr. Gregg was displayed, a curious figure in "shorts." On one side of the room two oars were hung and over the mantelpiece (littered with pipes) there were photographs of the "Mona Lisa" and Da Vinci's "Last Supper." The men in the room were embarrassed and silent. Under a strong light a minute undergraduate with enormous spectacles sat, white and trembling; it was obviously he who was to read the paper.

Mr. Gregg came forward heartily. "Why, Dune, this is quite splendid! The very man! Why, it is long since you've honoured our humble gathering. Baccy? That's right. Help yourself. Erdington's going to read to us about the Huns and stand a fire of questions afterwards, aren't you, Erdington?"

The youth in spectacles gulped.

"That's right. That's right. Comfortable now, Dune? Got all you want? That's right. Now we can begin, I think. Minutes of the last meeting, Stevens."

Olva placed himself in a corner and looked round the room. He found that most of the men were freshmen whose faces he did not know, but there, moving his fat body uneasily on a chair, was Bunning, and there, to his intense surprise, was Lawrence. That football hero was lounging with half-closed eyes in a large armchair. His broad back looked as though it would burst the wooden arms, and his plain, good-natured face beamed, through a cloud of smoke, upon the company. Below his short, light grey flannel trousers were bright purple socks. He had the body of a bullock—short, thick, broad, strong, thoroughly well calculated to withstand the rushes of oncoming three-quarters. Various freshmen flung timid glances at the hero every now and again; it was to them an event that they might have, for a whole hour, closely under their observation, this king among men.

Olva wondered at his presence. He remembered that Lawrence was taking a "pass" degree in History. He knew also that Lawrence somewhere in the depths of his slow brain had a thirst for knowledge and at the same time a certain assurance that he would never acquire any. His slow voice, his slow smile, the great, heavy back, the short thick legs attracted Olva; there was something simple and primeval here that appealed to the Dune blood. Moreover, since the afternoon when Olva had played against the Harlequins and covered himself with glory, Lawrence had shown a disposition to make friends. Old Lawrence might be stupid, but, as a background, he was the most important man in the College. His slow, lumbering body as it rolled along the Court was followed by the eyes of countless freshmen. His appearance on the occasion of a College concert was the signal for an orgy of applause. Cardillac might lead the College, but he was, nevertheless, of common clay. Lawrence was of the gods!

Swift contrast the fat and shapeless Bunning! As the tremulous and almost tearful voice of little Erdington continued the solemn and dreary exposition of the Huns, Olva felt increasingly that Bunning's eye was upon him. Olva had not seen the creature since the night of the revival, and he was irritated with himself for the persistence of his interest. The man's pluck had, in the first place, struck him, but now it seemed to him that they were, in some undefinable measure, linked together. As Olva watched him, half contemptuously, half sarcastically, he tried to pin his brain down to the actual, definite connection. It seemed ultimately to hang round that dreadful evening when they had been together; it was almost—although this was absurd—as though Bunning knew; but, in spite of the certain assurance of his ignorance Olva felt as he moved uneasily under Bunning's gaze that the man himself was making some claim upon him. It was evident that Bunning was unhappy; he looked as though he had not slept; his face was white and puffy, his eyes dark and heavy. He was paying no attention to the "Huns," but was trying, obviously, to catch Olva's eye. As the reading progressed Olva became more and more uneasy. It showed the things that must be happening to his nerves. He had now that sensation that had often come to him lately that some one was waiting for him outside the door. He imagined that the man next to him, a spotty, thin and restless freshman, would suddenly turn to him and say quite casually— "By the way, you killed Carfax, didn't you?" Above all he imagined himself suddenly rising in his place and saying—"Yes, gentlemen, this is all very well, very interesting I'm sure, but I killed Carfax."

His tortured brain was being driven, compelled to these utterances. Behind him still he felt that pursuing cloud; one day it would catch him and, out of the heart of it, there would leap . . .

And all this because Bunning looked at him. It was becoming now a habit—so general that it was instinctive—that, almost unconsciously, he should, at a point like this, pull at his nerves. "They are watching you; they are watching you. Don't let them see you like this; pull yourself together. . . ."

He did. Little Erdington's voice ceased. Mr. Gregg was heard saying: "It has always occurred to me that the Huns . . . " and then, after many speeches: "How does this point of view strike you, Erdington?"

It didn't strike Erdington very strongly, and there was no other person present who seemed to be struck in any very especial direction. The discussion, therefore, quickly flagged. Olva escaped Bunning's pleading eyes, found his gown amongst a heap in the corner, and avoiding Mr. Gregg's pressing invitation to stay, plunged down the stairs. Behind him, then, making his heart leap into his mouth, was a slow, thick voice.

"I say, Dune, what do you say to a little drink in my room after all that muck?" Above him, in the dark shadow of the stair, loomed Lawrence's thick body.

"I shall be delighted," Olva said.

Lawrence came lumbering down. He always spoke as though words were a difficulty to him. He left out any word that was not of vital necessity.

"Muck that-awful muck. What do they want gettin' a piffler like that kid in the glasses to read his ideas? Ain't got any—not one—no more 'an I have."

They reached the Court—it swam softly in the moonlight—stars burnt, here and there, in a trembling sky.

Lawrence put his great arm through Olva's. "Rippin' game that o' yours yesterday. Rippin'." He seemed to lick his lips over it as a gourmet over a delicate dish.

Lawrence pursued his slow thoughts.

"I say, you know, you—re one of these clever ones—thinkin' an' writin' an' all that—an' yet you play footer like an archangel—a blarsted archangel. Lucky devil!" He sighed heavily. "Every time I put on my footer boots," he pursued, "I say to myself, 'What you'd be givin', Jerry Lawrence, if you could just go and write a book! What you'd give! But it ain't likely—my spellin's somethin' shockin'."

Here there was interruption. Several men came rattling; laughing and shouting, down the staircase behind Lawrence and Olva.

"Oh, damn!" said Lawrence, slowly turning round upon them. Cardillac was there, also Bobby Galleon, Rupert Craven, and one or two more.

Cardillac shouted. "Hullo, Lawrence, old man. Is it true, as they say, that you've been sitting at the feet of our dearly beloved Gregg? How splendid for you!"

"I've been at our Historical Society hearin' about the Huns, and therefore there's compellin' necessity for a drink," Lawrence said, moving in the direction of his room.

"Oh! rot, don't go in yet. We're thinking of going round and paying Bunning a visit in another ten minutes. He's going to have a whole lot of men in for a prayer-meeting. Thompson's just brought word."

Thompson, a wretched creature in the Second Year, who had, during his first term, been of the pious persuasion and had since turned traitor, offered an eager assurance.

The news obviously tempted Lawrence. He moved his body slowly round.

"Well," he said slowly, then he turned to Olva. "You'll come?" he said.

"No, thanks," said Olva shortly. "Bunning's been ragged about enough. There's nothing the matter with the man."

Cardillac's voice was amused. "Well, Dune, I daresay we can get on without you," he said.

Lawrence said slowly, "Well, I don't know. P'raps it's mean on the man. I want a drink. I don't think I'm havin' any to-night, Cards."

Cardillac was sharper. "Oh, nonsense, Lawrence, come along. It doesn't do the man any harm."

"It frightens the fellow out of his wits," said Dune sharply. "You wouldn't like it yourself if you had a dozen fellows tumbling down upon your rooms and chucking your things out of the window."

Rupert Craven said: "Well, I'm off anyhow. Work for me." He vanished into the shadow.

Lawrence nodded. "Good-bye, Cards, old man. Go and play your old bridge or something—leave the wretched Bunnin' to his prayers."

Lawrence and Olva moved away.

III

The first thing that Lawrence said when they were lounging comfortably in his worn but friendly chairs hit Olva, expecting peace here at any rate, like a blow.

"Fellers have forgotten Carfax damn quick."

In that good-natured face there was no suspicion, but Olva seemed to see there a curiosity, even an excitement.

"Yes," he said, "they have."

"Fellers," said Lawrence again, "aren't clever in this College. They get their firsts in Science—little measly pups from Board Schools who don't clean their teeth—and there are one or two men who can row a bit and play footer a bit and play cricket a bit—I grant you all that—but they aren't clever—not what I call clever."

Olva waited for the development of Lawrence's brain.

"Now at St. Martin's they'll talk. They'll sit round a fire the whole blessed evenin' talkin'—about whether there's a God or isn't a God, about whether they're there or aren't there, about whether women are rotten or not, about jolly old Greece and jolly old Rome—I know. That's the sort o' stuff you could go in for—damn interestin'. I'd like to listen to a bit of it, although they'd laugh if they heard me say so, but what I'm gettin' at is that there ain't any clever fellers in this old bundle o' bricks, and Carfax's death proves it."

"How does it prove it?" asked Dune.

"Why, don't you see, they'd have made more of Carfax. Nobody said a blessed thing that any one mightn't have said."

Lawrence thought heavily for a moment or two, and then he brought out—

"Carfax was a stinker—a rotten fellow. That's granted, but there was more in it than just Carfax. Why, any one could give him a knock on the chin any day and there's no loss, but to have a feller killed in Sannet Wood where all those old Druids—"

As the words came from him Lawrence stopped.

"Druids?" said Olva.

"Why, yes. I wish I were a clever feller an' I could say what I mean, but if I'd been a man with a bit of grey matter that's what I'd have gone in for—those old stones, those old fellers who used to slash your throat to please their God. My soul, there's stuff there. They knew what fighting was—they'd have played footer with you. Ever since I was a tiny kid they've excited me, and if I'd been a brainy feller I'd have known a lot more, but the minute I start reactin' about them I get heavy, can't keep my eyes to it. But I've walked miles—often and often—to see a stone or a hill, don't yer know, and Sannet Wood's one o' the best. So, says I, when I hear about young Carfax bein' done for right there at the very place, I says to myself, 'You may look and look—hold your old inquests—collar your likely feller—but it wasn't a man that did it, and you'll have to go further than human beings if you fix on the culprit.'"

This was, in all probability, the longest speech that Lawrence had ever made in his life. He himself seemed to think so, for he added in short jerks: "It was those old Druids—got sick—o' the sight—o' Carfax's dirty body—bangin' about in their preserves—an' they gave him a chuck under the chin," and after that there was silence.

To Olva the effect of this was uncanny. He played, it seemed, a spiritual Blind Man's Buff. On every side of him things filled the air; once and again he would touch them, sometimes he would fancy that he was alone, clear, isolated, when suddenly something again would blunder up against him. And always with him, driving him into the bustle of his fellow men, flinging him, hurling him from one noise to another noise, was the terror of silence. Let him once be alone, once waiting in suspense, and he would hear. . . . What would he hear?

He felt a sudden impulse to speak.

"Do you know, Lawrence, in a kind of way I feel with you. I mean this—that if—I had, at any time, committed a murder or were indeed burdened by any tremendous breaking of a law, I believe it would be the consciousness of the Maker of the law that would pursue me. It sounds priggish, but I don't mean man. The laws that man has made nothing—subject to any temporary civilization, mere fences put up for a moment to keep the cattle in their proper fields. But the laws that God made—if you break one . . ."

Lawrence tuned heavily in his chair.

"Then you believe in God?"

"Yes, I believe in God."

After that there was silence. Both men felt uncomfortable. Led by some sudden, ungovernable impulse, they had both gone further than their slight acquaintance justified. Olva was convinced that he had made a fool of himself, that he had talked like a prig. Lawrence was groping hopelessly amongst a forest of dark thought for some little sensible thing that he might say. He found nothing and so relapsed, with false, uncomfortable easiness, into—

"I say, old man, have a drink."

The rest of that conversation concerned football.

CHAPTER VI

THE WATCHERS

I

He was running—running for his life. Behind stretched the long white road rising like a great bloated, warning finger out of the misty trees. Heavy cushions of grey cloud blotched the sky; through the mist ridges of ploughed field rose like bars.

The dog, Bunker, was running beside him, his tongue out, body solid grey against the lighter, floating grey around. His feet pattered beside his master, but his body appeared to edge away and yet to be held by some compelling force.

Olva was running, running. But not from Carfax. There in the wood it lay, the leg doubled under the body, the head hanging limply back. . . . But that was nought, no fear, no terror in that. It could not pursue, nor in its clumsy following, had it had such power, would there have been any horror. There was no sound in the world save his running and the patter of the dog's feet. Would the lights never come, those sullen streets and at last the grateful, welcome crowds?

He could see one lamp, far ahead of him, flinging its light forward to help him. If he might only reach it before the pursuer caught him. Then, behind him, oh! so softly, so gently, with a dreadful certainty, it came. If he did but once look round, once behold that Shadow, his defeat was sure. He would sink down there upon the road, the mists would crowd upon him, and then the awful end. He began to call out, his breath came in staggering gasps, his feet faltered.

"O, mercy, mercy—have mercy." He sank trembling to his knees.

"Dune, Dune, wake up! What's the matter? You've been making the most awful shindy. Dune, Dune!"

Slowly he came to himself. As his eyes caught the old familiar objects, the little diamond-paned window, the books, the smiling tenderness of "Aegidius," the last evening blaze lighting the room with golden splendour, he pulled himself together.

He had been sitting, he remembered now, in the armchair by the fire. Craven had come to tea. They had had their meal, had talked pleasantly enough, and then Olva had felt this overpowering desire for sleep come down upon him. He knew the sensation of it well enough by now, for his nights had often been crowded with waking hours, and this drowsiness would attack him at any time—in hall, in chapel, in lecture. Sometimes he had struggled against it, but to-day it had been too strong for him. Craven's voice had grown fainter and fainter, the room had filled with mist. He had made one desperate struggle, had seen through his hall-closed eyes that Craven was looking at a magazine and blowing, lazily, clouds of smoke from his pipe . . . then he had known no more.

Now, as he struggled to himself, he saw that Craven was standing over him, shaking him by the arm.

"Hullo," he said stupidly, "I'm afraid I must have dropped off. I'm afraid you must have thought me most frightfully rude."

Craven left him and went back to his chair.

"No," he said, "that's all right—only you did talk in the most extraordinary way."

"Did I?" Olva looked at him gravely. "What did I say?"

"Oh—I don't know—only you shouted a lot. You're overdone, aren't you? Been working too hard I expect." Then he added, slowly, "You were crying out about Carfax."

There was a long pause. The clock ticked, the light slowly faded, leaving the room in shadow. Craven's voice was uncomfortable. He said at last—

"You must have been thinking a lot about Carfax lately."

"What did I say?" asked Olva again.

"Oh, nothing." Craven turned his eyes away to the shadowy panes. "You were dreaming about a road—and something about a wood . . . and a matchbox."

"I've been sleeping badly." Olva got up, filled his pipe and relit it. "I expect, although we don't say much about it, the Carfax business has got on all our nerves. You don't look yourself, Craven."

He didn't. His careless, happy look had left him. Increasingly, every day, Olva seemed to see in him a likeness to his mother and sister. The eyes now were darker, the tines of the mouth were harder.

Meanwhile so strong bad the dream's impression been that Olva could not yet disentangle it from his waking thoughts. He was in his room and yet the white road stretched out of it—somewhere there by the bookcase—oil through the mist into the heart of the dark wood.

He had welcomed during these last days Craven's advances towards friendship, partly because he wanted friends now, and partly, he was beginning now to recognize, there was, in the back of his mind, the lingering memory of the kind eyes of Margaret Craven. He perceived, too, that here was sign enough of change in him—that he who had, from his earliest days, held himself proudly, sternly aloof from all human companionship save that of his father, should now, so readily and eagerly, greet it. Craven had been proud of him, eager to be with him, and had shown, in his artless opinions of men and things, the simplest, most innocent of characters.

"Time to light up," said Olva. The room had grown very dark.

"I must be going."

Olva noticed at once that there was a new note in Craven's voice. The boy moved, restlessly, about the room.

"I say," he brought out at last, laughing nervously, "don't go asleep when I'm in the room again. It gives one fits."

Both men were conscious of some subtle, vague impression moving in the darkness between them.

Olva answered gravely, "I've been sticking in at an old paper I've been working on—no use to anybody, and I've been neglecting my proper work for it, but it's absorbed me. That's what's given me such bad nights, I expect."

"I shouldn't have thought," Craven answered slowly, "that anything ever upset you; I shouldn't have thought you had any nerves. And, in any case, I didn't know you had thought twice about the Carfax business."

Olva turned on the electric light. At the same moment there was a loud knock on the door.

Craven opened it, showing in the doorway a pale and flustered Bunning. Craven looked at him with a surprised stare, and then, calling out good-bye to Olva, walked off.

Bunning stood hesitating, his great spectacles shining owl-like in the light.

Dune didn't want him. He was, he reflected as he looked at him, the very last person whom he did want. And then Bunning had most irritating habits. There was that trick of his of pushing up his spectacles nervously higher on to his nose. He bad a silly shrill laugh, and he had that lack of tact that made him, when you had given him a shilling's worth of conversation and confidence, suppose that you had given him half-a-crown's worth and expect that you would very shortly give him five shillings' worth. He presumed on nothing at all, was confidential when he ought to have been silent, and gushing when he should simply have thanked you with a smile. Nothing, moreover, to look at. He had the kind of complexion that looks as though it would break into spots at the earliest opportunity. His clothes fitted him badly and were dusty at the knees; his hair was of no colour nor strength whatever, and he bit his nails. His eyes behind his spectacles were watery and restless, and his linen always looked as though it had been quite clean yesterday and would be quite filthy to-morrow.

And yet Olva, as he looked at him seated awkwardly in a chair, was surprisingly, unexpectedly touched. The creature was so obviously sincere. It was indeed poor Bunning's only possible "leg," his ardour. He would willingly go to the stake for anything. It was the actual death and sacrifice that mattered—and Bunning's life was spent in marching, magnificently and wholeheartedly, to the sacrificial altars and then discovering that he had simply been asked to tea.

Now it was evident that he wanted something from Olva. His tremulous eyes bad, as they gazed at Dune across the room, the dumb worship of a dog adoring its master.

"I hear," he said in that husky voice that always sounded as though he were just swallowing the last crumbs of a piece of toast, "that you stopped Cardillac and the others coming round to my rooms the other night. I can't tell you how I feel about it."

"Rot," said Olva brusquely. "If you were less of an ass they wouldn't want to come round to your rooms so often."

"I know," said Bunning. "I am an awful ass." He pushed his spectacles up his nose. "Why did you stop them coming?" he asked.

"Simply," said Olva, "because it seems to me that ten men on to one is a rotten poor game."

"I don't know," said Bunning, still very husky, "If a man's a fool he gets rotted. That's natural enough. I've always been rotted all my life. I used to think it was because people didn't understand me—now I know that it really is because I am an ass."

Strangely, suddenly, some of the burden that bad been upon Olva now for so long was lifted. The atmosphere of the room that had lain upon him so heavily was lighter—and he seemed to feel the gentle withdrawing of that pursuit that now, ever, night and day, sounded in his ears.

And what, above all, had happened to him? He flung his mind back to a month ago. With what scorn then would he have glanced at Bunning's ugly body—with what impatience have listened to his pitiful confessions. Now he said gently—

"Tell me about yourself."

Bunning gulped and gripped the baggy knees of his trousers.

"I'm very unhappy," he said at last desperately—"very. And if you hadn't come with me the other night to hear Med-Tetloe—I'm sure I don't know why you did—I shouldn't have come now—"

"Well, what's the matter?"

Bunning's mouth was full of toast. "It was that night—that service. I was very worked up and I went round afterwards to speak to him. I could see, you know, that it hadn't touched you at all. I could see that, and then when I went round to see him he hadn't got anything to say—nothing that I wanted—and—suddenly—then—at that moment—I felt it was all no good. It was you, you made me feel like that—"

"I?"

"Yes. If you hadn't gone—like that—it would have been different. But when you—the last man in College to care about it-went and gave it its chance I thought that would prove it. And then when I went to him he was so silly, Med-Tetloe I mean. Oh! I can't describe it but it was just no use and I began to feel that it was all no good. I don't believe there is a God at all—it's all been wrong—I don't know what to do. I don't know where to go. I've been wretched for days, not sleeping or anything. And then they come and rag me—and—and—the Union men want me to take Cards round for a Prayer Meeting—and—and—I wouldn't, and they said. . . . Oh! I don't know, I don't know what to do—I haven't got any-thing left!"

And here, to Olva's intense dismay, the wretched creature burst into the most passionate and desperate tears, putting his great hands over his face, his whole body sobbing. It was desolation—the desolation of a human being who had clutched desperately at hope after hope, who had demanded urgently that he should be given something to live for and had had all things snatched from his hands.

Olva, knowing what his own loneliness was, and the terror of it, understood. A fortnight ago he would have hated the scene, have sent Bunning, with a cutting word, flying from the room, never to return.

"I say, Bunning, you mustn't carry on like this—you're overdone or something. Besides, I don't understand. What does it matter if you have grown to distrust Med-Tetloe and all that crowd. They aren't the only people in the world—that isn't the only sort of religion."

"It's all I had. I haven't got anything now. They don't want me at home. They don't want me here. I'm not clever. I can't do anything. . . . And now God's gone. . . . I think I'll drown myself."

"Nonsense. You mustn't talk like that—God's never gone."

Bunning dropped his hands, looked up, his face ridiculous with its tear-stains.

"You think there's a God?"

"I know there's a God."

"Oh!" Bunning sighed.

"But you mustn't take it from me, you know. You must think it out for yourself. Everybody has to."

"Yes—but you matter—more to me than—any one."

"I?"

"Yes." Bunning looked at the floor and began to speak very fast. "You've always seemed to me wonderful—so different from every one else. You always looked—so wonderful. I've always been like that, wanted my hero, and I haven't generally been able to speak to them—my heroes I mean. I never thought, of course, that I should speak to you. And then they sent me that day to you, and you came with me—it was so wonderful—I've thought of nothing else since. I don't think God would matter if you'd only let me come to see you sometimes and talk to you—like this."

"Don't talk that sort of rot. Always glad to see you. Of course you may come in and talk if you wish."

"Oh! you're so different—from what I thought. You always looked as though you despised everybody— and now you look—Oh! I don't know—but I'm afraid of you—"

The wretched Bunning was swiftly regaining confidence. He was now, of course, about to plunge a great deal farther than was necessary and to burden Olva with sell-revelations and the rest.

Olva hurriedly broke in—

"Well, come and see me when you want to. I've got a lot of work to do before Hall. But we'll go for a walk one day. . . ."

Bunning was at once flung back on to his timid self. He pushed his spectacles back, blushed, nearly tumbled over his chair as he got up, and backed confusedly out of the room.

He tried to say something at the door—"I can't thank you enough. . ." he stuttered and was gone.

As the door closed behind him, swiftly Olva was conscious again of the Pursuit. . . .

He turned to the empty room—"Leave me alone," he whispered. "For pity's sake leave me alone."

The silence that followed was filled with insistent, mysterious urgency.

II

Craven did not come that night to Hall. Galleon had asked him and Olva to breakfast-the next morning. He did not appear.

About two o'clock in the afternoon a note was sent round to Olva's rooms. "I've been rather seedy. Just out for a long walk—do you mind my taking Bunker? Send word round to my rooms if you mind.—R. C." Craven had taken Bunker out for walks before and had grown fond of the dog. There was nothing in that. But Olva, as he stood in the middle of his room with the note in his hand, was frightened.

The result of it was that about five o'clock on that afternoon Olva paid his second visit to the dark house in Rocket Road. His motives for going were confused, but he knew that at the back of them was a desire that he should find Margaret Craven, with her grave eyes, waiting for him in the musty little drawing-room, and that Mrs. Craven, that mysterious woman, should not be there. The hall, when the old servant had admitted him, once again seemed to enfold him in its darkness and heavy air with an almost active purpose. It breathed with an actual sound, almost with a melody . . . the "Valse Triste" of Sibelius, a favourite with Olva, seemed to him now to be humming its thin spiral note amongst the skins and Chinese weapons that covered the walls. The House seemed to come forward, on this second occasion, actively, personally. . . . His wish was gratified. Margaret Craven was alone in the dark, low-ceilinged drawing-room, standing, in her black dress, before the great deep fireplace, as though she had known that he would come and had been awaiting his arrival.

"I know that you will excuse my mother," she said in her grave, quiet voice. "She is not very well. She will be sorry not to have seen you." Her hand was cool and strong, and, as he held it for an instant, he was strangely conscious that she, as well as the House, had moved into more intimate relation with him since their last meeting.

They sat down and talked quietly, their voices sounding like low notes of music in the heavy room. He was conscious of rest in the repose of her figure, the pale outline of her face, the even voice, and above all the grave tenderness of her eyes. He was aware, too, that she was demanding from him something of the same kind; he divined that for her, too, life had been no easy thing since they last met and that she wanted now a little relief before she must return. He tried to give it her.

All through their conversation he was still conscious in the dim rustle that any breeze made in the room of that thin melody that Sibelius once heard. . . .

"I hope that Mrs. Craven is not seriously ill?

"No. It is one of her headaches. Her nerves are very easily upset. There was a thunder-storm last night. . . . She has never been strong since father died."

"You will tell her how sorry I am."

"Thank you. She is wonderfully brave about it. She never complains—she suffers more than we know, I think. I don't think this house is good for her. Father died here and her bedroom now is the room where he died. That is not good for her, I'm sure. Rupert and I both are agreed about it, but we cannot get her to change her mind. She can be very determined."

Yes—Olva, remembering her as she sat so sternly before the fire, knew that she could be determined.

"And I am afraid that your brother isn't very well either."

She looked at him with troubled eyes. "I am distressed about Rupert. He has taken this death of his friend so terribly to heart. I have never known him morbid about anything before. It is really strange because I don't think he was greatly attached to Mr. Carfax. There were things I know that he didn't like."

"Yes. He doesn't look the kind of fellow who would let his mind dwell on things. He looks too healthy."

"No. He came in to see us for an hour last night and sat there without a word. I played to him—he seemed not to hear it. And generally he cares for music."

"I'm afraid"—their eyes met and Olva held hers until he had finished his sentence—"I'm afraid that it must seem a little lonely and gloomy for you here—in this house—after your years abroad."

She looked away from him into the fire.

"Yes," she said, speaking with sudden intensity. "I hate it. I have hated it always—this house, Cambridge, the life we lead here. I love my mother, but since I have been abroad something has happened to change her. There is no confidence between us now. And it is lonely because she speaks so little—I am afraid she is really very ill, but she refuses to see a doctor. . . ."

Then her voice was softer again, and she leant forward a little towards him. "And I have told you this, Mr. Dune, because if you will you can help me—all of us. Do you know that she liked you immensely the other even big? I have never known her take to any one at once, so strongly. She told me afterwards that you had done her more good than fifty doctors—just your being there—so that if, sometimes, you could come and see her—"

He did not know what it was that suddenly, at her words, brought the terror back to him. He saw Mrs. Craven so upright, so motionless, looking at him across the room—with recognition, with some implied claim. Why, he had spoken scarcely ten words to her. How could he possibly have been of any use to her? And then, afraid lest his momentary pause had been noticeable, he said eagerly—

"It is very kind of Mrs. Craven to say that. Of course I will come if she really cares about it. I am not a man of many friends or many occupations. . . ."

She broke in upon him—

"You could be if you cared. I know, because Rupert has told me. They all think you wonderful, but you don't care. Don't throw away friends, Mr. Dune—one can be so lonely without them."

Her voice shook a little and he was suddenly afraid that she was going to cry. He bent towards her.

"I think, perhaps, we are alike in that, Miss Craven. We do not make our friends easily, but they mean a great deal to us when they come. Yes, I am lonely and I am a little tired of bearing my worries alone, in silence. Perhaps I can help you to stand this life a little better if I tell you that—mine is every bit as hard."

She turned to him eyes that were filled with gratitude. Her whole body seemed to be touched with some new glow. Into the heart of their consciousness of the situation that had arisen between them there came, sharply, the sound of a shutting door. Then steps in the hall.

"That's Rupert," she said.

They both rose as he came into the room. He stood back in the shadow for a moment as though surprised at Olva's presence. Then he came forward very gravely.

"I've found something of yours, Dune," he said. It lay, gleaming, in his hand. "Your matchbox."

Dune drew a sharp breath. Then he took it and looked at it.

"Where did you find it?"

"In Saunet Wood. Bunker and I have been for a walk there. Bunker found it."

As the three of them stood there, motionless, in the middle of the dark room, Olva caught, through the open door, the last sad fading breath of the "Valse Triste."

CHAPTER VII

TERROR

I

That night the cold fell, like a plague, upon the town. It came, sweeping across the long low flats, crisping the dark canals with white frosted ice, stiffening the thin reeds at the river's edge, taking each blade of grass and holding it in its iron hand and then leaving it an independent thing of cold and shining beauty. At last it blew in wild gales down the narrow streets, throwing the colour of those grey walls against a sky of the sharpest blue, making of each glittering star a frozen eye, carrying in its arms a round red sun that it might fasten it, like a frosted orange, against its hard blue canopy.

Already now, at half-past two of the afternoon, there were signs of the early dusk. The blue was slowly being drained from the sky, and against the low horizon a faint golden shadow soon to burn into the heart of the cold blue, was hovering.

Olva Dune, turning into the King's Parade, was conscious of crowds of people, of a gaiety and life that filled the air with sound. He checked sternly with a furious exercise of self-control his impulse to creep back into the narrow streets that he had just left.

"It's an Idea," he repeated over and over, as he stood there. "It's an Idea. . . . You are like any one else— you are as you were . . . before . . . everything. There is no mark—no one knows."

For it seemed to him that above him, around him, always before him and behind him there was a grey shadow, and that as men approached him this shadow, bending, whispered, and, as they came to him, they flung at him a frightened glance . . . and passed.

If only he might take the arm of any one of those bright and careless young men and say to him, "I killed Carfax—thus and thus it was." Oh! the relief! the lifting of the weight! For then—and only then—this pursuing Shadow, so strangely grave, not cruel, but only relentless, would step back. Because that confession—how clearly he knew it!—was the thing that God demanded. So long as he kept silence he resisted the Pursuer—so long as he resisted the Pursuer he must fly, he must escape—first into Silence, then into Sound, then back again to Silence. Somewhere, behind his actual consciousness: there was the knowledge that, did he once yield himself, life would be well, but that yielding meant Confession, Renunciation, Devotion. It was not because it was Carfax that he had killed, but it was because it was God that had spoken to him, that he fled.

A fortnight ago he would have been already defeated—the Pursuer should have caught him, bound him, done with him as he would. But now—in that same instant that young Craven had looked at him with challenge in his eyes, in that instant also he, Olva, had looked at Margaret.

In that silence, yesterday evening, in the dark drawing-room the two facts had together leapt at him— he loved Margaret Craven, he was suspected by Rupert Craven. Love had thus, terribly, grimly, and yet so wonderfully, sprung into his heart that had never, until now, known its lightest touch. Because of it— because Margaret Craven must never know what he had done—he must fight Craven, must lie and twist and turn. . . . His soul must belong to Margaret Craven, not to this terrible, unperturbed, pursuing God.

All night he had fought for control. A very little more and he would rush crying his secret to the whole world; slowly he had summoned calm back to him. Rupert Craven should be defeated; he would, quietly, visit Sannet Wood, face it in its naked fact, stand before it and examine it—and fight down once and for all this imagination of God.

Those glances that men flung upon him, that sudden raising of the eyes to his face . . . a man greeted him, another man waved his hand always this same suspicion . . . the great grey shadow that bent and whispered in their ears.

He saw, too, another picture. High above him some great power was seated, and down to earth there bent a mighty Hand. Into this Hand very gently, very tenderly, certain figures were drawn—Mrs. Craven, Margaret, Rupert, Bunning, even Lawrence. Olva was dragging with him, into the heart of some terrible climax, these so diverse persons; he could not escape now—other lives were twisted into the fabric of his own.

And yet with this certainty of the futility of it, he must still struggle . . . to the very end.

On that cold day the world seemed to stand, as men gather about a coursing match, with hard eyes and jeering faces to watch the hopeless flight. . . .

II

He fetched Banker from the stable where he was kept and set off along the hard white road. He had behaved very badly to Bunker, a but the dog showed no signs of delight at his release. On other days when he had been kept in his stable for a considerable time he had gone mad with joy and jumped at his master, wagging his whole body in excitement. Now he walked very slowly by Olva's side, a little way behind him; when Olva spoke to him he wagged his tail, but as though it were duty that impelled it.

The air grew colder aid colder—slowly now there had stolen on to the heart of the blue sky white pinnacles of cloud—a dazzling whiteness, but catching, mysteriously, the shadow of the gold light that heralded the setting sun. These clouds were charged with snow; as they hung there they seemed to radiate from their depths an even more piercing coldness. They hung above Olva like a vast mountain range and had in their outline so sharp and real an existence that they were part of the hard black horizon, rising, immediately, out of the long, low, shivering flats.

There was no sound in all the world; behind him, sharply, the Cambridge towers bit the sky—before him like a clenched hand was the little wood.

The silence seemed to have a rhythm and voice of its own so that if one listened, quite clearly the tramp of a marching army came over the level ground. Always an army marching—and when suddenly a bird rose from the canal with a sharp cry the tramping was caught, with the bird, for an instant, into the air, and then when the cry was ended sank down again. The wood enlarged; it lay upon the cold land now like a man's head; a man with a cap. Spaces between the trees were eyes and it seemed that he was lying behind the rim of the world and leaning his head upon the edge of it and gazing. . . .

Bunker suddenly stopped and looked up at his master.

"Come on," Olva turned on to him sharply.

The dog looked at him, pleading. Then in Olva's dark stern face he seemed to see that there was no relenting—that wood must be faced. He moved forward again, but slowly, reluctantly. All this nonsense that Lawrence had talked about Druids. We will soon see what to make of that. And yet, in the wood, it did seem as though there were something waiting. It was now no longer a man's head—only a dark, melancholy band of trees, dead black now against the high white clouds.

There had risen in Olva the fighting spirit. Fear was still there, ghastly fear, but also an anger, a rage. Why should he be thus tormented? What had he done? Who was Carfax that the slaying of him should be so unforgettable a sin? Moreover, had it been the mere vulgar hauntings of remorse, terrors of a frightened conscience, he could have turned upon himself the contempt that any Dune must deserve for so ignoble a submission.

But here there were other things—some-thing that no human resolution could combat. He seized then eagerly on the things that he could conquer—the suspicions of Rupert Craven, the rivalry of Cardillac, the confidences of Bunning, . . . the grave tenderness of Margaret Craven . . . these things he would clutch and hold, let the Pursuing Spirits do what they would.

As he entered the dark wood a few flakes of snow were falling. He knew where the Druid Stones lay. He had once been shown them by some undergraduate interested in such things. They lay a little to the right, below the little crooked path and above the Hollow.

The wood was not dripping now—held in the iron hand of the frost the very leaves on the ground seemed to be made of metal; the bare twisted branches of the trees shone with frosty—the earth crackled beneath his foot and in the wood's silence, when he broke a twig with his boot the sound shot into the air and rang against the listening stillness.

He looked at the Hollow, Bunker close at his heels. He could see the spot where he had first stood, talking to Carfax—there where the ferns now glistened with silver. There was the place where Carfax had fallen. Bunker was smelling with his head down at the ground. What did the dog remember? What had Craven meant when he said that Bunker had found the matchbox?

He stood silently looking down at the Hollow. In his heart now there was no terror. When, during these last days, he had been fighting his fear it had always seemed to him that the heart of it lay in this Hollow. He had always seen the dripping fern, smelt the wet earth, heard the sound of the mist falling from the trees. Now the earth was clear and hard and cold. The great white mountains drove higher into the sky, very softly and gently a few white flakes were falling.

With a great relief, almost a sigh of thank-fulness, he turned back to the Druids' Stones. There they were—two of them standing upright, stained with lichen, grey and weather-beaten, one lying flat, hollowed a little in the centre. The ferns stood above them and the bare branches of the trees crossed in strange shapes against the sky.

Here, too, there was a peaceful, restful silence. No more was God in these quiet stones than He had been in that noisy theatrical Revival Meeting—Lawrence was wrong. Those old religions were dead. No more could the Greek Gods pass smiling into the temples of their worshippers, no more Wodin, Thor and the rest may demand their bloody sacrifice.

These old stones are dead. The Gods are dead—but God? . . .

He stayed there for a while and the snow fell more heavily. The golden light had faded, the high white clouds had swallowed the blue. There would soon be storm.

In the wood—strangest of ironies—there had been peace.

Now he started down the road again and was conscious, as the wood slipped back into distance, of some vague alarm.

III

The world was now rapidly transformed. There had been promised a blaze of glory, but the sun, red and angry, had been drowned by the thick grey clouds that now flooded the air—dimly seen for an instant outlined against the grey—then suddenly non-existent, leaving a world like a piece of crumpled paper white and dark to all its boundaries.

The snow fell now more swiftly but always gently, imperturbably—almost it might seem with the whispering intention of some important message.

Olva was intensely cold. He buttoned his coat tightly up to his ears, but nevertheless the air was so biting that it hurt. Bunker, with his head down, drove against the snow that was coming now ever more thickly.

The peace that there had been in the little wood was now utterly gone. The air seemed full of voices. They came with the snow, and as the flakes blew more closely against his face and coat there seemed to press about him a multitude of persons.

He drove forward, but this sense of oppression increased with every step. The wood had been swallowed by the storm. Olva felt like a man who has long been struggling with some vice; insidiously the temptation has grown in force and power—his brain, once so active in the struggle, is now dimmed and dulled. His power of resistance, once so vigorous, is now confused—confusion grows to paralysis—he can only now stare, distressed, at the dark temptation, there have swept over him such strong waters that struggle is no longer of avail—one last clutch at the vice, one last desperate and hateful pleasure, and he is gone. . . .

Olva knew that behind him in the storm the Pursuit was again upon him. That brief respite in the wood had not been long granted him. The snow choked him, blinded him, his body was desperately cold, his soul trembling with fear. On every side he was surrounded—the world had vanished, only the thin grey body of his dog, panting at his side, could be dimly seen.

God had not been in the wood, but God was in the storm. . . .

A last desperate resistance held him. He stayed where he was and shouted against the blinding snow.

"There is no God. . . . There is no God."

Suddenly his voice sank to a whisper. "There is no God," he muttered.

The dog was standing, his eyes wide with terror, his feet apart, his body quivering.

Olva gazed into the storm. Then, desperately, he started to run. . . .

CHAPTER VIII

REVELATION OF BUNNING (I)

I

On that evening the College Debating Society exercised its mind over the question of Naval Defence.

One gentleman, timid of voice, uncertain in wit, easily dismayed by the derisive laughter of the opposite party, asserted that "This House considers the Naval policy of the present Government fatal to the country's best interests." An eager politician, with a shrill voice and a torrent of words, denied this statement. The College, with the exception of certain gentlemen destined for the Church (they had been told by their parents to speak on every possible public occasion in order to be ready for a prospective pulpit), displayed a sublime and somnolent indifference. The four gentlemen on the paper had prepared their speeches beforehand and were armed with notes and a certain nervous fluency. For the rest, the question was but slightly assisted. The prospective members of the Church thought of many things to say until they rose to their feet when they could only remember "that the last gentleman's speech bad been the most preposterous thing they had ever had the pleasure of listening to—and that, er—er—the Navy was all right, and, er—if the gentleman who had spoken last but two thought it wasn't, well, all they—er—could say was that it reminded them—er—of a story they had once heard (here follows story without point, conclusion or brevity)—and—er—in fact the Navy was all right. . . ."

The Debate, in short, was languishing when Dune and Cardillac entered the room together. Here was an amazing thing.

It was well known that only last night Cardillac and Dune had both been proposed for the office of President of the Wolves. The Wolves, a society of twelve founded for the purpose of dining well and dressing beautifully, was by far the smartest thing that Saul's possessed. It was famous throughout the University for the noise and extravagance of its dinners, and you might not belong to it unless you had played for the University on at least one occasion in some game or another and unless, be it understood, you were, in yourself, quite immensely desirable. Towards the end of every Christmas term a President for the ensuing year was elected; he must be a second year man, and it was considered by the whole college that this was the highest honour that the gods could possibly, during your stay at Cambridge, confer upon you. Even the members of the Christian Union, horrified though they were by the amount of wine that was drunk on dining occasions and the consequent peril to their own goods and chattels, bowed to the shining splendour of the fortunate hero. It had never yet been known that a President of the Wolves should also be a member of the Christian Union, but one must never despair, and nets, the most attractive and genial of nets, were flung to catch the great man.

On the present occasion it had been generally understood that Cardillac would be elected without any possible opposition. Dune had not for a moment occurred to any one. He had; during his first term, when his football prowess had passed, swinging through the University, been elected to the Wolves, but he had only attended one dinner and had then remained severely and unpleasantly sober. There was no other possible rival to Cardillac, to his distinction, his power of witty and malicious after-dinner speaking, his wonderful clothes, his admirable football, his haughty indifference. He would of course be elected.

And then, some three weeks ago, this wonderful, unexpected development of Olva Dune had startled the world. His football, his sudden geniality (he had been seen, it was asserted, at one of Med-Tetloe's revival meetings with, of all people in the world, Bunning), his air of being able to do anything whatever if he wished to exert himself, here was a character indeed—so wonderful that it was felt, even by the most patriotic of Saulines, that he ought, in reality, to have belonged to St. Martin's.

It became at once, of course, a case of rivalry between Dune and Cardillac, and it was confidently expected that Dune would be victorious in every part of the field.

Cardillac had reigned for a considerable period and there were many men to whom he had been exceedingly offensive. Dune, although he admitted no one to closer intimacy, was offensive never. If, moreover, you had seen him play the other day against the Harlequins, you could but fall down on your knees and worship. Here, too, he rivalled Cardillac. Tester, Buchan, and Whymper were quite certain of their places in the University side—Whymper because he was the greatest three-quarter that Cambridge had had for many seasons, and Tester and Buchan because they had been at Fettes together and Buchan had played inside right to Tester's outside since the very tenderest age; they therefore understood one another backward. There remained then only this fourth place, and Cardillac seemed certain enough . . . until Dune's revival. And now it depended on Whymper. He would choose, of the two men, the one who suited him the better. Cardillac had played with him more than had Dune. Cardillac was safe, steady, reliable. Dune was uncertain, capricious, suddenly indifferent. On the other hand not Whymper himself could rival the brilliance of Dune's game against the Harlequins. That was in a place by itself—let him play like that at Queen's Club in December and no Oxford defence could stop him.

So it was argued, so discussed. Certain, at any rate, that Dune's recrudescence threatened the ruin of Cardillac's two dearest ambitions, and Cardillac did not easily either forget or forgive.

And yet behold them now, gravely, the gaze of the entire company, entering together, sitting together by the fire, watching with serious eyes the clumsy efforts of an unhappily ambitious Freshman to make clear his opinions of the Navy, the Government and the British Islands generally—only, ultimately, producing a tittering, stammering apology for having burdened so long with his hapless clamour, the Debate.

II

Olva liked Cardillac—Cardillac liked Olva. They both in their attitude to College affairs saw beyond the College gates into the wide and bright world. Cardillac, when it had seemed that no danger could threaten either his election to the Wolves or the acquisition of his Football Blue, had regarded both honours quietly and with indifference. It amazed him now when both these Prizes were seriously threatened that he should still appreciate and even seek out Dune's company.

Had it been any other man in the College he would have been a very active enemy, but here was the one man who had that larger air, that finer style whose gravity was beautiful, whose soul was beyond Wolves and Rugby football, whose future in the real world promised to be of a fine and highly ordered kind. Cardillac wished eagerly that these things might yet be his, but if he were to be beaten, then, of all men in the world, let it be by Dune. In his own scant, cynical estimate of his fellow-beings Dune alone demanded a wide and appreciative attention.

To Olva on this evening it mattered but little where he was or what he did. The snow had ceased to fall, and now, under a starry sky, lay white and glistening clear; but still with him storm seemed to hover, its snow beating his body, its fury yieling him no respite.

And now there was no longer any doubt. He faced it with the most matter-of-fact self-possession of which he was capable. Some-thing was waiting for his surrender. He figured it, sitting quietly back in the reading-room, listening to the Debate, watching the faces around him, as the tracing of some one who was dearly loved. There was nothing stranger in it all than his own certainty that the Power that pursued him was tender. And here he crossed the division between the Real and the Unreal, because his present consciousness of this Power was as actual as his consciousness of the chairs and tables that filled the reading-room. That was the essential thing that made the supreme gulf between himself and his companions. It was not because he had murdered Carfax but because he was now absolutely conscious of God that he was so alone. He could not touch his human companions, he could scarcely see them. It was through this isolation that God was driving him to confession. Now, in the outer Court, huge against the white dazzling snow, the great shadow was hovering, its head piercing the stars, its arms outstretched. Let him surrender and at once there would be infinite peace, but with surrender must come submission, confession . . . with confession he must lose the one thing that he desired—Margaret Craven . . . that he might go and talk to her, watch her, listen to her voice. Meanwhile he must not think. If he allowed his brain, for an instant, to rest, it was flooded with the sweeping consciousness of the Presence—always he must be doing something, his football, his companions, and often at the end of it all, calmly, quietly, betrayed—hearing above all the clatter that he might make the gentle accents of that Voice. He remembered that peace that he had had in St. Martin's Chapel on the day of the discovery of the body. What he would give to reclaim that now!

Meanwhile he must battle; must quiet Craven's suspicions, must play football, join company with men who seemed to him now like shadows. As he glanced round at them—at Lawrence, Bunning, Galleon Cardillac—they seemed to have far less existence than the grey shadow in the outer Court. Sounds passed him like smoke—the lights grew faint in his eyes . . . he was being drawn out into a world that was all of ice—black ice stretching to every horizon; on the edge of it, vast against the night sky, was the Grey Figure, waiting.

"Come to Me. Tell Me that you will follow Me. I spoke to you in the wood. You have broken My law. . . ."

"Lot of piffle," he heard Cardillac's voice from a great distance. "These freshers are always gassing." The electric light, seen through a cloud of tobacco smoke, came slowly back to him, dull globes of colour.

"It's so hot—I'm cutting," he whispered to Cardillac, and slipped out of the room.

He climbed to his room, flung back his door and saw that his light was turned on.

Facing him, waiting for him, was Bunning.

III

"If you don't want me—" he began with his inane giggle.

"Sit down." Olva pulled out the whisky and two siphons of soda. "If I didn't want you I'd say so."

He filled himself a strong glass of whisky and soda and began feverishly to drink.

Bunning sat down.

"Don't be such a blooming fool. Take off your gown if you're going to stop."

Bunning meekly took off his gown. His spectacles seemed so large that they swallowed up the rest of his face; the spectacles and the enormous flat-toed boots were the principal features of Bunning's attire. He sat down again and gazed at Olva with the eyes of a devoted dog. Olva looked at him. Over Bunning's red wrists the brown ends of a Jaeger vest protruded from under the shirt.

"I say, why don't you dress properly?"

"I don't know—" began Bunning.

"Well, the sleeves of your vest needn't come down like that. It looks horribly dirty. Turn 'em up."

Bunning, blushing almost to tears, turned them back.

"There's no need to make yourself worse than you are, you know," Olva finished his whisky and poured out some more. "Why do you come here? . . . I'm always beastly to you."

"As long as you let me come—I don't mind how beastly you are."

"But what do you get from it?"

Bunning looked down at his huge boots.

"Everything. But it isn't that—it is that, without being here, I haven't got anything else."

"Well, you needn't wear such boots as that—and your shirts and things aren't clean. . . . You don't mind my telling you, do you?"

"No, I like it, Nobody's ever told me."

Here obviously was a new claim for intimacy and this Olva hurriedly disavowed.

"Oh! It's only for your own good, you know. Fellows will like you better if you're decently dressed. Why hasn't any one ever told you?"

"They'd given me up at home." Bunning heaved a great sigh.

"Why? Who are your people?"

"My father's a parson in Yorkshire. They're all clergymen in my family—uncles, cousins, everybody—my elder brother. I was to have been a clergyman."

"Was to have been? Aren't you going to be one now?"

"No—not since I met you."

"Oh, but you mustn't take such a step on my account. I don't want to prevent you. I've nothing to do with it. I should think you'd make a very good parson."

Olva was brutal. He felt that in Bunning's moist devoted eyes there was a dim pain. But he was brutal because his whole soul revolted against sentimentality, not at all because his soul revolted against Bunning.

"No, I shouldn't make a good parson. I never wanted to be one really. But when your house is full of it, as our house was, you're driven. When it wasn't relations it was all sorts of people in the parish—helpers and workers—women mostly. I hated them."

Here was a real note of passion! Bunning seemed, for an instant, to be quite vigorous.

"That's why I'm so untidy now," Bunning went desperately on; "nobody cared how I looked. I was stupid at school, my reports were awful, and I was a day boy. It is very bad for any one to be a day boy—very!" he added reflectively, as though he were recalling scenes and incidents.

"Yes?" said Olva encouragingly. He was being drawn by Bunning's artless narration away from the Shadow. It was still there, its arm outstretched above the snowy court, but Bunning seemed, in some odd way, to intervene.

"I always wanted to find God in those days. It sounds a stupid thing to say, but they used to speak about Him—mother and the rest—just as though He lived down the street. They knew all about Him and I used to wonder why I didn't know too. But I didn't. It wasn't real to me. I used to make myself think that it was, but it wasn't."

"Why didn't you talk to your mother about it?—

"I did. But they were always too busy with missions and things. And then there was my elder brother. He understood about God and went to all the Bible meetings and things, and he was always so neat-never dirty—I used to wonder how he did it . . . always so neat."

Bunning took off his great spectacles and wiped them with a very dirty handkerchief.

"And had you no friends?"

"None—nobody. I didn't want them after a bit. I was afraid of everybody. I used to go down all the side-streets between school and home for fear lest I should meet some one. I was always very nervous as a boy—very. I still am."

"Nervous of people?"

"Yes, of everybody. And of things, too—things. I still am. You'd be surprised. . . . It's odd because none of the other Bunnings are nervous. I used to have fancies about God."

"What sort of fancies?"

"I used to see Him when I was in bed like a great big shadow, all up against the wall. A grey shadow with his head ever so high. That's how I used to think of Him. I expect that all sounds nonsense to you."

"No, not at all!" said Olva.

"I think they thought me nearly an idiot at home—not sane at all. But they didn't think of me very often. They used to apologise for me when people came to tea. I wasn't clever, of course—that's why they thought I'd make a good parson."

He paused—then very nervously he went on. "But now I've met you I shan't be. Nothing can make me. I've always watched you. I used to look at you in chapel. You're just as different from me as any one can be, and that's why you're like God to me. I don't want you to be decent to me. I think I'd rather you weren't. But I like to come in sometimes and hear you say that I'm dirty and untidy. That shows that you've noticed."

"But I'm not at all the sort of person to make a hero of," Olva said hurriedly. "I don't want you to feel like that about we. That's all sentimentality. You mustn't feel like that about anybody. You must stand on your own legs."

"I never have," said Burning, very solemnly, "and I never will. I've always had somebody to make a hero of. I would love to die for you, I would really. It's the only sort of thing that I can do, because I'm not clever. I know you think me very stupid."

"Yes, I do," said Olva, "and you mustn't talk like a schoolgirl. If we're friends and I let you come in here, you mustn't let your vest come over your cuffs and you must take those spots off your waistcoat, and brush your hair and clean your nails, and you must just be sensible and have a little humour. Why don't you play football?"

"I can't play games, I'm very shortsighted."

"Well, you must take some sort of exercise. Run round Parker's Piece or something, or go and run at Fenner's. You'll get so fat."

"I am getting fat. I don't think it matters much what I look like."

"It matters what every one looks like. And now you'd better cut. I've got to go out and see a man."

Burning submissively rose. He said no more but bundled out of the door in his usual untidy fashion. Olva came after him and banged his "oak" behind him. In Outer Court, looking now so vast and solemn in the silence of its snow, Bunning, stopping, pointed to the grey buildings that towered over them.

"It was against a wall like that that I used to imagine God—on a night like this—you'll think that very silly." He hurriedly added, "There's Marshall coming. I know he'll be at me about those Christian Union Cards. Good-night." He vanished.

But it was not Marshall. It was Rupert Craven. The boy was walking hurriedly, his eyes on the ground. He was suddenly conscious of some one and looked up. The change in him was extraordinary. His eyes had the heavy, dazed look of one who has not slept for weeks. His face was a yellow white, his hair unbrushed, and his mouth moved restlessly. He started when he saw Olva.

"Hallo, Craven. You're looking seedy. What's the matter?"

"Nothing, thanks. . . . Good-night."

"No, but wait a minute. Come up to my rooms and have some coffee. I haven't seen you for days."

A fortnight ago Craven would have accepted with joy. Now he shook his head.

"No, thanks. I'm tired: I haven't been sleeping very well."

"Why's that? Overwork?"

"No, it's nothing. I don't know why it is."

"You ought to see somebody. I know what not sleeping means."

"Why? . . . Are you sleeping badly?" Craven's eyes met Olva's.

"No, I'm splendid, thanks. But I had a bout of insomnia years ago. I shan't forget it."

"You look all right." Cravan's eyes were busily searching Olva's face. Then suddenly they dropped.

"I'm all right," he said hurriedly. "Tired, that's all."

"Why do you never come and see me now?"

"Oh, I will come—sometime. I'm busy."

"What about?"

Olva stood, a stern dark figure, against the snow.

"Oh, just busy." Craven suddenly looked up as though he were going to ask Olva a question. Then he apparently changed his mind, muttered a good-night and disappeared round the corner of the building.

Olva was alone in the Court. From some room came the sound of voices and laughter, from some other room a piano—some one called a name in Little Court. A sheet of stars drew the white light from the snow to heaven.

Olva turned very slowly and entered his black stairway.

In his heart he was crying, "How long can I stand this? Another day? Another hour? This loneliness. . . . I must break it. I must tell some one. I must tell some one."

As he entered his room he thought that he saw against the farther wall an old gilt mirror and in the light of it a dark figure facing him; a voice, heavy with some great overburdening sorrow, spoke to him.

"How terrible a thing it is to be alone with God!"

CHAPTER IX

REVELATION OF BUNNING (II)

I

The next day the frost broke, and after a practice game on the Saul's ground, in preparation for a rugby match at the end of the week, Olva, bathed and feeling physically a fine, overwhelming fitness, went to see Margaret Craven.

This sense of his physical well-being was extraordinary. Mentally he was nearly beaten, almost at the limit of his endurance. Spiritually the catastrophe hovered more closely above him at every advancing moment, but, physically, he had never, in all his life before, felt such magnificent health. He had been sleeping badly now for weeks. He had been eating very little, but he felt no weariness, no faintness. It was as though his body were urging upon him the importance of his resistance, as though he were perceiving, too, with unmistakable clearness the cleavage that there was between body and soul. And indeed this vigour did give him an energy to set about the numberless things that he had arranged to fill every moment of his day—the many little tinkling bells that he had set going to hide the urgent whisper of that other voice. He carried his day through with a rush, a whirl, so that he might be in bed again at night almost before he had finished his dressing in the morning—no pause, no opportunity for silence. . . .

And now he must see Margaret Craven, see her for herself, but also see her to talk to her about her brother. How much did Rupert Craven know? How much—and here was the one tremendous question—had he told his sister? As Olva waited, once again, in the musty hall, saw once more the dim red glass of the distant window, smelt again the scent of oranges, his heart was beating so that he could not hear the old woman's trembling voice. How would Margaret receive him? Would there be in her eyes that shadow of distrust that he always saw now in Rupert's? His knees were trembling and he had to stay for an instant and pull himself together before he crossed the drawing-room threshold.

And then he was, instantly, reassured. Margaret was alone in the dim room, and as she came to meet him he saw in her approach to him that she had been wanting him. In her extended hands he found a welcome that implied also a need. He felt, as he met her and greeted her and looked again into the grave, tender eyes that he had been wanting so badly ever since he had seen them last, that there was nothing more wonderful than the way that their relationship advanced between every meeting. They met, exchanged a word or two and parted, but in the days that separated them their spirits seemed to leap together, to crowd into lonely hours a communion that bound them more closely than any physical intimacy could do.

"Oh! I'm so glad you've come. I had hoped it, wanted it."

He sat down close to her, his dark eyes on her face.

"You're in trouble? I can see."

She bent her eyes gravely on the fire, and as slowly she tried to put together the things that she wished to say he felt, in her earnest thoughtfulness, a rest, a relief, so wonderful that it was like plunging his body into cool water after a long and arid journey.

"No, it is nothing. I don't want to make things more overwhelming than they are. Only, it is, I think, simply that during these last days when mother and Rupert have both been ill, I have been overwhelmed."

"Rupert?"

"Yes, we'll come to him in a moment. You must remember," she smiled up at him as she said it, "that I'm not the least the kind of person who makes the best of things—in fact I'm not a useful person at all. I suppose being abroad so long with my music spoiled me, but whatever it is I seem unable to wrestle with things. They frighten me, overwhelm me, as I say . . . I'm frightened now."

He looked up at her last word and caught a corner reflection in the old gilt mirror—a reflection of a multitude of little things; silver boxes, photograph frames, old china pots, little silk squares, lying like scattered treasures from a wreck on a dark sea.

"What are you frightened about?"

"Well, there it is—nothing I suppose. Only I'm not good at managing sick people, especially when there's nothing definitely the matter with them. It's a case with all three of us—a case of nerves."

"Well, that's as serious a thing as any other disease."

"Yes, but I don't know what to do with it. Mother lies there all day. She seldom speaks, she scarcely eats anything. She entirely refuses to have a doctor. But worse than that is the extraordinary feeling that she has had during this last week about Rupert. She refuses to see him," Margaret Craven finally brought out.

"Refuses?"

"Yes, she says that he is altered to her. She says that he will not let her alone, that he is imagining things. Poor Rupert is most terribly distressed. He is imagining nothing. He would do anything for her, he is devoted to her."

"Since when has she had this idea?"

"You remember the day that you came last? when Rupert came in and had found your matchbox. It began about then. . . . Of course Rupert has not been well—he has never been well since that dreadful death of Mr. Carfax, and certainly since that day when you were here I think that he's been worse—strange, utterly unlike himself, sleeping badly, eating nothing. Poor, poor Rupert, I would do anything for him, for them both, but I am so utterly, utterly useless, What can I do?" she finally appealed to him.

"You said once," he answered her slowly, "that I could help you. If you still feel that, tell me, and I will do anything, anything. You know that I will do anything."

They came together, in that terrible room, like two children out of the dark. He suddenly caught her hand and she let him hold it. Then, very gently, she withdrew it.

"I think that you can make all the difference," she answered slowly. "Mother often speaks of you. I told you before that she wants so much to see you, and if you would do that, if you would go up, for just a little time, and sit with her, I believe you would soothe her as no one else can. I don't know why I feel that, but I know that she feels it too. You are restful," she said suddenly, with a smile, flung up at him.

And again, as on the earlier occasion, he shrank from the thing that she asked him. He had felt, from the very moment this afternoon that he had entered the house, that that thing would be asked of him. Mrs. Craven wanted him. He could feel the compulsion of her wish drawing him through walls and floors and all the obstructions of the world.

"Of course I'll go," he said.

"Ah! that will help. It would be so good of you. Poor mother, it's lonely for her up there all day, and I know that she thinks about things, about father, and it's not good for her. You might perhaps say a word too about Rupert. I cannot imagine what it is that she is feeling about him." She paused, and then with a sigh, rising from their chair, longingly brought out, "Oh! but for all of us! to get away—out of this house, out of this place, that's the thing we want!"

She stood there in her black dress, so simply, so appealingly before him, that it was all that he could do not to catch her in his arms and bold her. He did indeed rise and stand beside her, and there in silence, with the dim room about them, the oppressive silence so ominous and sinister, they came together with a closeness that no earlier intercourse had given them.

Olva seemed, for a short space, to be relieved from his burdens. For them both, so young, so helpless against powers that were ruthless in the accomplishment of wider destinies, they were allowed to find in these silent minutes a brief reprieve.

Then, with the sudden whirring and shrill clatter of an ancient clock, action began again, but before the striking hour had entirely died away, he said to her, "Whatever happens, we are, at any rate, friends. We can snatch a moment together even out of the worst catastrophe."

"You're afraid . . . ?" Her breath caught, as she flung a look about the room.

"One never knows."

"It is all so strange. There in Dresden everything was so happy, so undisturbed, the music and one's friends; it was all so natural. And now—here—with Rupert and mother—it's like walking in one's sleep."

"Well, I'll walk with you," he assured her.

But indeed that was exactly what it was like, he thought, as he climbed the old and creaking stairs. How often had one dreamed of the old dark house, the dusty latticed windows, the stairs with the gaping boards, at last that thin dark passage into which doors so dimly opened, that had black chasms at either end of it, whose very shadows seemed to demand the dripping of some distant water and the shudder of some trembling blind. In a dream too there was that sense of inevitability, of treading unaccustomed ways with an assured, accustomed tread that was with him now. The old woman who had conducted him stopped at a door, hidden by the dusk, and knocked. She opened it and wheezed out—

"Mr. Dune, m'am;" and then, standing back for him to pass, left him inside.

As the door closed he was instantly conscious of an overwhelming desire for air, a longing to fling open the little diamond-paned window. The ceiling was very low and a fierce fire burned in the fireplace. There was little furniture, only a huge white bed hovered in the background. Olva was conscious of a dark figure lying on a low chair by the fire, a figure that gave you instantly those long white hands and those burning eyes and gave you afterwards more slowly the rest of the outline. But its supreme quality was its immobility. That head, that body, those hands, never moved, only behind its dark outline the bright fire crackled and flung its shadows upon the wall.

"I am sorry that you are not so well."

Mrs. Craven's dark eyes searched his face. "You are restful to me. I like you to come. But I would not intrude upon your time."

Olva said, "I am very glad to come if I can be of any service. If there is anything that I can do."

The eyes seemed the only part of her body that lived. It was the eyes that spoke. "No, there is nothing that any one can do. I do not care for talking. Soon I will be downstairs again, I hope. It is lonely for my daughter."

"There is Rupert."

At the mention of the name her eyes were suddenly sheathed. It was like the instant quenching of some light. She did not answer him.

"Tell me about yourself. What you do, what you care about . . . your life."

He told her a little about his home, his father, but he had a strange, overwhelming conviction that she already knew. He felt, also, that she regarded these things that he told her as preliminaries to something else that he would presently say. He paused.

"Yes?" she said.

"I am tiring you. I have talked enough. It is time for me to be back in College."

She did not contradict him. She watched him as he said good-bye. For one moment he touched her chill, unresponsive hand, for an instant their eyes, dark, sombre, met. The thought flew to his brain, "My God, how lonely she is . . ." and then, "My God, how lonely I am." Slowly and quietly he closed the door behind him.

II

That night the Shadow was nearer, more insistent; the closer it came the more completely was the real world obscured. This obscurity was now shutting oil from him everything; it was exactly as though his whole body bad been struck numb so that he might touch, might hold, but could feel nothing. Again it was as though he were confined in a damp, underground cell and the world above his head was crying out with life and joy. In his hand was the key of the door; he had only to use it.

Submission—to be taken into those arms, to be told gently what he must do, and then—Obedience— perhaps public confession, perhaps death, struggling, ignominious death . . . at least, never again Margaret Craven, never again her companionship, her understanding, never again to help her and to feel that warm sure clasp of her hand. What would she say, what would she do if she were told? That remained for him now the one abiding question. But he could not doubt what she would do. He saw the warmth fading from the eyes, the hard stern lines settling about the mouth, the cold stiffening of her whole body. No, she must never know, and if Rupert discovered the truth, he, Olva, must force him, for his sister's sake, to keep silence. But if Rupert knew he would tell his sister, and she would believe him. No use denials then.

And on the side of it all was the Shadow, with him now, with him in the room.

All things betray Thee Who betrayest Me.

The line from some poem came to him. It was true, true. His life that had been the life of a man was now the life of a Liar—Liar to his friends, Liar to Margaret, Liar to all the world—so his shuddering soul cowered there, naked, creeping into the uttermost corner to escape the Presence.

If only for an hour he might be again himself—might shout aloud the truth, boast of it, triumph in it, be naked in the glory of it. Day by day the pressure had been increased, day by day his loneliness had grown, day by day the pursuit had drawn closer.

And now he hardly recognized the real from the false. He paced his room frantically. He felt that on the other side of the bedroom door there was terror. He had turned on all his lights; a furious fire was blazing in the grate; beyond the windows cold stars and an icy moon, but in here stifling heat.

When Bunning (the clocks were striking eleven) came blinking in upon him he was muttering—"Let me go, let me go. I killed him, I tell you. I'm glad I killed him. . . . Oh! Let me alone! For pity's sake let me alone! I can't confess! Don't you see that I can't confess? There's Margaret. I must keep her—afterwards when she knows me better I'll tell her."

As he faced Bunning's staring glasses, the thought came to Him, "Am I going mad?—Has it been too much for me?—Mad?"

He stopped, wheeled round, caught the table with both hands, and leaned over to Bunning, who stood, his mouth open, his cap and gown still on.

Olva very gravely said: "Come in, Bunning. Shut the door. 'Sport' it. That's right. Take off your gown and sit down."

The man, still staring, white and frightened, sat down.

Olva spoke slowly and very distinctly: "I'm glad you've come. I want to talk to you. I killed Carfax, you know." As he said the words he began slowly to come back to himself from the Other World to this one. How often, sleeping, waking, had he said those words! How often, aloud, in his room, with his door locked, had he almost shouted them!

He was not now altogether sure whether Bunning were really there or no. His spectacles were there, his boots were there, but was Bunning there? If he were not there. . . .

But he was there. Olva's brain slowly cleared and, for the first time for many weeks, he was entirely himself. It was the first moment of peace that he had known since that hour in St. Martin's Chapel.

He was quiet, collected, perfectly calm. He went over to the window, opened it, and rejoiced in the breeze. The room seemed suddenly empty. Five minutes ago it had been crowded, breathless. There was now only Bunning.

"It was so awfully hot with that enormous fire," he said.

Bunning's condition was peculiar. He sat, his large fat face white and streaky, beads of perspiration on his forehead, his hands gripping the sides of the armchair. His boots stuck up in the most absurd manner, like interrogation marks. He watched Olva's face fearfully. At last he gasped—

"I say, Dune, you're ill. You are really—you're overdone. You ought to see some one, you know. You ought really, you ought to go to bed." His words came in jerks.

Olva crossed the room and stood looking down upon him.

"No, Bunning, I'm perfectly well. . . . There's nothing the matter with me. My nerves have been a bit tried lately by this business, keeping it all alone, and it's a great relief to me to have told you."

The fact forced itself upon Bunning's brain. At last in a husky whisper: "You . . . killed . . . Carfax?" And then the favourite expression of such weak souls as he: "Oh! my God! Oh! my God!"

"Now look here, don't get hysterical about it. You've got to take it quietly as I do. You said the other day you'd do anything for me. . . . Well, now you've got a chance of proving your devotion."

"My God! My God!" The boots feebly tapped the floor.

"I had to tell somebody. It was getting on my nerves. I suppose it gives you a kind of horror of me. Don't mind saying so if it does."

Bunning, taking out a grimy handkerchief, wiped his forehead. He shook his head without speaking.

Olva sat down in the chair opposite him and lit his pipe.

"I want to tell somebody all about it. You weren't really, I suppose, the best person to tell. You're a hysterical sort of fellow and you're easily frightened, but you happened to come in just when I was rather worked up about it. At any rate you've got to face it now and you must pull yourself together as well as you can. . . . Move away from the fire, if you're hot."

Bunning shook his head.

Olva continued: "I'm going to try to put it quite plainly to you, the Carfax part of it I mean. There are other things that have happened since that I needn't bother you with, but I'd like you to understand why I did it."

"Oh! my God!" said Bunning. He was trembling from head to foot and his fat hands rattled on the woodwork of the chair and his feet rattled on the floor.

"I met Carfax first at my private school—a little, fat dirty boy he was then, and fat and dirty he's been ever since. I hated him, but I was always pleasant to him. He wasn't worth being angry with. He always did rotten things. He knew more filthy things than the other boys, and he was a bully—a beastly bully. I think he knew that I hated him, but we were on perfectly good terms. I think he was always a little afraid of me, but it's curious to remember that we never had a quarrel of any kind, until the day when I killed him."

Olva paused and asked Bunning to have a drink. Bunning, gazing at him with desperate eyes, shook his head.

"Then we went on to Rugby together. It's odd how Fate has apparently been determined to hammer out our paths side by side. Carfax grew more and more beastly. He always did the filthiest things and yet out of it all seemed to the world at large a perfectly decent fellow. He was clever in that way. I am not trying to defend myself. I'm making it perfectly straightforward and just as it really was. He knew that I knew him better than anybody, and as we went on at Rugby I think that his fear of me grew. I didn't hate him so much for being Carfax, but rather as standing for all sorts of rotten things. It didn't matter to me in the least whether he was a beast or not, I'm a beast myself, but it did matter that he should smile about it and have damp hands. When I touched his hand I always wanted to hit him.

"I've got a very sudden temper, all my family are like that—calm most of the time and then absolutely wild. I hated him more up here at College than I'd hated him at school. He developed and still his reputation was just the same, decent fellows like Craven followed him, excused him; he had that cheery manner. . . . Hating him became a habit with me. I hated everything that he did—his rolling walk down the Court, his red colour, his football . . . and then he ruined that fellow Thompson. That was a poor game, but no one seemed to think anything of it . . . and indeed he and I seemed to be very good friends. He used to sneer at me behind my back, I know, but I didn't mind that. Any one's at liberty to sneer if they like. But he was really afraid of me . . . always.

"Then at last there was this girl that he set about destroying. He seduced her, promised her marriage. I knew all about it, because she used to be rather a friend of mine. I warned her, but she was absolutely infatuated—wouldn't hear of anything that I had to say, thought it all jealousy. She wasn't the kind of girl who could stand disgrace. . . . She came to him one day and told him that she was going to have a baby. He laughed at her in the regular old conventional way . . . and that very afternoon, after he had seen her, he met me—there in Sannet Wood.

"He began to boast about it, told me jokingly about the way that he'd 'shut her mouth,' as he called it . . . laughed . . . I hit him. I meant to hit him hard, I hated him so; I think that I wanted to kill him. All the accumulated years were in that blow, I suppose; at any rate, I caught him on the chin and it broke his neck and he dropped . . . that's all."

Olva paused, finished his drink, and ended with—

"There it is—it's simple enough. I'm not in the least sorry I killed him. I've no regrets; he was better out of the world than in it, and I've probably saved a number of people from a great deal of misery. I thought at first that I should be caught, but they aren't very sharp round here and there was really nothing to connect me with it. But there were other things—there's more in killing a man than the mere killing. I haven't been able to stand the loneliness—so I told you."

The last words brought him back to Bunning, a person whom he had almost forgotten. A sudden pity for the man's distress made his voice tender. "I say, Running, I oughtn't to have told you. It's been too much for you. But if you knew the relief that it is to me. . . . Though, mind you, if it's on your conscience, if it burdens you, you must 'out' with it. Don't have any scruples about me. But it needn't burden you. You hadn't any-thing to do with it. You were here and I told you. That's all. I've shown you that I want you as a friend."

For answer the creature burst suddenly into tears, hiding his face in his sleeve, as small boys hide their faces, and choking out desperately—

"Oh! my God! Oh! my God!"

CHAPTER X

CRAVEN

I

That evening Olva was elected President of the Wolves. It was a ceremony conducted with closed doors and much drinking of wine, by a committee of four and the last reigning President who had the casting vote. The College waited in suspense and at eleven o'clock it was understood that Dune had been elected.

According to custom, on the day following in "Hall" Olva would be cheered by the assembled undergraduates whilst the gods on the dais smiled gently and murmured that "boys will be boys."

Meanwhile the question that agitated the Sauline world was the way that Cardillac would take it. "If it had been any one else but Dune . . ." but it couldn't have been any one else. There was no other possible rival, and "Cards," like the rest of the world, bowed to Dune's charm. The Dublin match, to be played now in a fortnight's time, would settle the football question. It was generally expected that they would try Dune in that match and judge him finally then on his play. There was a good deal of betting on the matter, and those who remembered his earlier games said that nothing could ever make Dune a reliable player and that it was a reliable player that was wanted.

When Olva came into "Hall" that evening he was conscious of two pairs of eyes, Craven's and Bunning's. On either side of the high vaulted hall the tables were ranged, and men, shouting, waving their glasses, lined the benches. Olva's place was at the end farthest from the door and nearest the High Table, and he had therefore the whole room to cross. He was smiling a little, a faint colour in his cheeks. At his own end of the table Craven was standing, silent, with his eyes gravely fixed upon Olva's face. Half-way down the hall there was Bunning, and Olva could see, as he passed up the room, that the man was trembling and was pressing his hands down upon the table to hold his body still.

When Olva had sat down and the cheering had passed again into the cheerful hum that was customary, the first voice that greeted him was Cardillac's.

"Congratulations, old man. I'm delighted."

There was no question of Cardillac's sincerity. Craven was sitting four places lower down; he had turned the other way and was talking eagerly to some man on his farther side—but the eyes that had met Olva's two minutes before had been hostile.

Cardillac went on: "Come in to coffee afterwards, Dune; several men are coming in."

Olva thanked him and said that he would. The world was waiting to see how "Cards" would take it, and, beyond question, "Cards" was taking it very well. Indeed an observer might have noticed that "Cards" was too absorbed by the way that Dune was "taking it" to "take it" himself consciously at all. Olva's aloof surveying of the world about him, as a man on a hill surveys the town in the valley, made of "Cards'" last year and a half a gaudy and noisy thing. He had thought that his attitude had been nicely adjusted, but now he saw that there were still heights to be reached—perhaps in this welcome that he was giving to Dune's success he might attain his position. . . . Not, in any way, a bad fellow, this Cardillac—but obsessed by a self-conscious conviction that the world was looking at him; the world never looks for more than an instant at self-consciousness, but it dearly loves self-forgetfulness, for that implies a compliment to itself.

Afterwards, in Cardillac's handsome and over-careful rooms, there was an attempt at depth. The set—Lawrence, Galleon, Craven and five or six more—never thought about Life unless drink drove them to do so, and drink drove them to-night. A long, thin man, Williamson by name, with a half-Blue for racquets and a pensive manner, had a favourite formula on these occasions: "But think of a rabbit now . . ." only conveying by the remark that here was a proof of God's supreme, astounding carelessness. "You shoot it, you know, without turning a hair (no joke, you rotter), and it breeds millions a week . . . and—does it think about it, that's what I want to know? Where's its soul?

"Hasn't got a soul. . . ."

"Well, what is the soul, anyway?"

There you are-the thing's properly started, and the more the set drinks the vaguer it gets until finally it goes happily to bed and wakes with a headache and a healthy opinion that "Religion and that sort of stuff is rot" in the morning. That is precisely as far as intellect ever ventured in Saul's. There may have been quaint obscure fellows who sported their oaks every night and talked cleverly on ginger-beer, but they were not admitted as part of the scheme of things. . . . Saulines, to quote Lawrence, "are not clever."

They were not especially clever to-night, thought Olva, as he sat in the shadow away from the light of the fire and watched them sitting back in enormous armchairs, with their legs stretched out, blowing wreaths of smoke into the air, drinking whiskies and sodas . . . no, not clever.

Craven, the shadows blacker than ever under his eyes, was on the opposite side of the room from Olva. He sat with his head down and was silent.

"Think of a rabbit now," said Williamson.

"I suppose," said Galleon, who was not gifted, "that they're happy enough."

"Yes, but what do they make of it all?"

At this moment Craven suddenly burst in with "Where's Carfax?"

This question was felt by every one to be tactless. Elaborately, with great care and some considerable effort, Carfax had been forgotten—forgotten, it seemed, by every one save Craven. He had been forgotten because his death did not belong to the Cambridge order of things, because it raised unpleasant ideas, and made one morbid and neurotic. It had, in fact, nothing in common with cold baths, marmalade, rugby football, and musical comedy.

On the present occasion the remark was especially unpleasant because Craven had made it in so odd a manner. During the last few weeks it had been very generally noticed that Craven had not been himself—so pleasant and healthy a fellow he had always been, but now this Carfax business was too much for him. "Look out for young Craven" had been the general warning, implied if not expressed. Persons who threatened to be unusual were always marked down in Cambridge.

And now Craven had been unusual—"Where's Carfax?" . . . What a dreadful thing to say and how tactless! The note, moreover, in Craven's voice sounded a danger. There was something in the air as though the fellow might, at any moment, burst into tears, fire a pistol into the air, or jump out of the window! So unpleasant, and Carfax was much more real, even now, than an abstract rabbit.

"Dear boy," said Cardillac, easily, "Carfax is dead. We all miss him—it was a beastly, horrible affair, but there's no point in dwelling on things; one only gets morbid, and morbidity isn't what we're here for."

"It's all very well," Craven was angrily muttering, "but it's scandalous the way you forget a man. Here he was, amongst the whole lot of you, only a month or so ago and he was a friend of every one's. And then some brute kills him—he's done for—and you don't care a damn . . . it's beastly—it makes one sick."

"Where do you think he is, Craven?" Olva asked quietly from his shadowy corner.

Craven flung up his head. "Perhaps you can tell us," he cried. There was such hostility in his voice that the whole room was startled. Poor Craven! He really was very unwell. The sight of his tired eyes and white cheeks, the shadow of his hand quivering on his knee—here were signs that all was not as it should be. Gone, now, at any rate, any possibility of a comfortable evening. Craven said no more but still sat there with his head banging, his only movement the shaking of his hand.

Cardillac tried to bring ease back again, Williamson once more started his rabbits, but now there was danger in that direction. Conversation fell, heavily, helplessly, to the ground. Some man got up to go and some one else followed him. It was the wrong moment for departure for they had drunk enough to make it desirable to drink more, but to escape from that white face of Craven's was the thing—out into the air.

At last Craven himself got up. "I must be off," he said heavily.

"So must I," Olva said, coming forward from his corner. Craven flung him a frightened glance and then passed stumbling out of the door.

Olva caught him up at the bottom of the dark stairs. He put a hand on Craven's trembling arm and held him there.

"I want to talk to you, Craven. Come up to my room."

Craven tried to wrench his arm away. "No, I'm tired. I want to go to bed."

"You haven't been near me for weeks. Why?"

"Oh, nothing—let me go. I'll come up another time."

"No, I must talk to you—now. Come." Olva's voice was stern—his face white and hard.

"No—I won't."

"You must. I won't keep you long. I have something to tell you."

Craven suddenly ceased to struggle. He gazed straight into Olva's eyes, and the look that he gave him was the strangest thing—something of terror, something of anger, a great wonder, and even—strangest of all!—a struggling affection.

"I'll come," he said.

In Olva's room he stood, a disturbed figure facing the imperturbability of the other man with restless eyes and hands that moved up and down against his coat. Olva commanded the situation, with stern eyes he seemed to be the accuser. . . .

"Sit down—fill a pipe."

"No, I won't sit—what do you want?"

"Please sit. It's so much easier for us both to talk. I can't say the things that I want to when you're standing over me. Please sit down."

Craven sat down.

Olva faced him. "Now look here, Craven, a little time ago you came and wished that we should see a good deal of one another. You came in here often and you took me to see your people. You were charming . . . I was delighted to be with you."

Olva paused—Craven said nothing.

"Then suddenly, for no reason that I can understand, this changed. Do you remember that afternoon when you had tea with me here and I went to sleep? It was after that—you were never the same after that. And it has been growing worse. Now you avoid me altogether—you don't speak to me if you can help it. I'm not a man of many friends and I don't wish to lose one without knowing first what it is that I have done. Will you tell me what it is?"

Craven made no answer. His eyes passed restlessly up and down the room as though searching for some way of escape. He made little choking noises in his throat. When Olva had had no answer to his question, he went gravely on—

"But it isn't only your attitude to me that matters, although I do want you to explain that. But I want you also to tell me what the damage is. You're most awfully unwell. You're an utterly different man—

changed entirely during the last week or two, and we've all noticed it. But it doesn't only worry us here; it worries your mother and sister too. You've no right to keep it to yourself."

"There's nothing the matter."

"Of course there is. A man doesn't alter in a day for nothing, and I date it all from that evening when you had tea with me, and I can't help feeling that it's something that I can clear up. If it is anything that I can do, if I can clear your bother up in any way, you have only to tell me. And," he added slowly, "I think at least that you owe me an explanation of your own personal avoidance of me. No man has any right to drop a friend without giving his reasons. You know that, Craven."

Craven suddenly raised his weary eyes. "I never was a friend of yours. We were acquaintances—that's all."

"You made me a friend of your mother and sister. I demand an explanation, Craven."

"There is no explanation. I'm not well—out of condition."

"Why?"

"Why is a fellow ever out of condition? I've been working too hard, I suppose. . . . But you said you'd got something to tell me. What have you got to tell me?"

"Tell me first what is troubling you."

"No."

"You refuse?"

"Absolutely."

"Then I have nothing to tell you."

"Then you brought me in here on a lie. I should never have come if—"

"Yes?"

"If I hadn't thought you had something to tell me."

"What should I have to tell you?"

"I don't know . . . nothing."

There was a pause, and then with a sudden surprising force, Craven almost appealed—

"Dune, you can help me. You can make a great difference. I am ill; it's quite true. I'm not myself a bit and I'm tortured by imaginations—awful things. I suppose Carfax has got on my nerves and I've had absurd fancies. You can help me if you'll just answer me one question—only one. I don't want to know anything else, I'll never ask you anything else—only this. Where were you on the afternoon that Carfax was murdered?"

He brought it out at last, his hands gripping the sides of his chair, all the agonized uncertainty of the last few weeks in his voice. Olva faced him, standing above him, and looking down upon him.

"My dear Craven—what an odd question—why do you want to know?"

"Well, finding your matchbox like that—there in Sannet Wood—and I know you must have lost it just about then because I remember your looking for it here. I thought that perhaps you might have seen somebody, had some kind of suspicion. . . ."

"Well, I was, as a matter of fact, there that very afternoon. I walked through the wood with Bunker—rather late. I met no one during the whole of the time."

"No one?"

"No one."

"You have no suspicion?"

"No suspicion."

The boy relapsed from his eagerness into his heavy dreary indifference. His lips were working. Olva seemed to catch the words—"Why should it be I? Why should it be I?" Olva came over to him and placed his hand on his shoulder.

"Look here, old man, I don't know what's the matter with you, but it's plain enough that you've got this Carfax business on your nerves—drop it. It does no good—it's the worst thing in the world to brood about. Carfax is dead—if I could help you to find his murderer I would—but I can't."

Craven's whole body was trembling under Olva's hand. Olva moved back to his chair.

"Craven, listen to me. You must listen to me." Then, speaking very slowly he brought out-"I have a right to speak to you—a great right. I wish to marry your sister."

Craven started up from his chair.

"No, no," he cried. "You! Never, so long as I can prevent it."

"You have no right to say that," Olva answered him sternly, "until you have given me your reasons. I don't know that she cares a pin about me—I don't suppose that she does. But she will. I'm going to do my very best to marry her."

Craven broke away to the middle of the room. His body was shaking with passion and he flung out his hand as though to ward off Olva from him.

"You to marry my sister! My God, I will prevent it—I will tell her—" He caught himself up suddenly.

"What will you tell her?"

Then Craven collapsed. He stood there, rocking on his feet, his hands covering his face.

"It's all too awful," he moaned. "It's all too awful."

For a wonderful moment Olva felt that he was about to tell Craven everything. A flood of words rose to his lips—he seemed, for an instant, to be rising with a great joyous freedom, as did Christian when he had dropped his burden, to a new honesty, a high deliverance.

Then he remembered Margaret Craven.

"You take my advice, Craven, and get your nerves straight. They're in a shocking condition."

Craven went to the door and turned.

"You can tell nothing?"

"Nothing."

"I will never rest until I know who murdered Carfax."

He closed the door behind him and was gone.

CHAPTER XI

FIFTH OF NOVEMBER

I

That attempt to make Craven speak his mind was Olva's last plunge into the open. He saw now, with a clarity that was like the sudden lifting of some blind before a lighted window, that he had been beguiled, betrayed. He had thought that his confession to Bunning would stay the pursuit. He saw now that it was the Pursuer Himself who had instigated it. With that confession the grey shadow had drawn nearer, had made one degree more certain the ultimate capitulation.

For Bunning was surely the last person to be told—with every hour that became clearer. There were now about four weeks before the end of term. The Dublin match was to be on the first Tuesday of December, two days before every one went down, and between the two dates—this 5th of November and that 2nd of December—the position must be held. . . .

The terror of the irresistible impulse now never left Olva. He had told Bunning in a moment of uncontrol—what might he not do now at any time? At one instant to be absolutely silent seemed the only resource, at the next to rush out and take part in all the life about him. Were he silent he was tortured by the silence, if he flung himself amongst his fellow men every hour threatened self-betrayal.

What, moreover, was happening in the house in Rocket Road? Craven was only waiting for certainty and at any moment some chance might give him what he needed. What did Mrs. Craven know?

Margaret . . . Margaret . . . Margaret—Olva took the thought of her in his hand and held it like a sword, against the forces that were crowding in upon him.

The afternoon of November 5 was thick with fog so that the shops were lighted early and every room was dim and unreal, and a sulphurous smell weighted the air. After "Hall" Olva came back to his room and found Bunning, his white face peering out of the foggy mist like a dull moon from clouds, waiting for him. All day there had hung about Olva heavy depression. It had seemed so ugly and sinister a world— the fog had been crowded with faces and terror, and the dreadful overpowering impression of unreality that had been increasing with every day now took from his companions all life and made of them grinning masks. He remembered Margaret's cry, "It is like walking in a dream," and echoed it. Surely it was a dream! He would wake one happy morning and find that he had invited Craven and Carfax to breakfast, and he would hear them, whilst he dressed, talking together in the outer room, and, later, he would pass Bunning in the Court without knowing him. He would be introduced one day to Margaret Craven and find the house in which she lived a charming comfortable place, full of light and air, with a croquet lawn at the back of it, and Mrs. Craven, a nice ordinary middle-aged woman, stout possibly and fond of gossip. And instead of being President of the Wolves and a person of importance in the College he would be once again his old self, knowing nobody, scornful of the whole world and of the next world as well. And this brought him up with a terrible awakening. No, that old reality could never be real again, for that old reality meant a world without God. God had come and had turned the world into a nightmare . . . or was it only his rebellion against God that had so made it? But the nightmare was there, the awful uncertainty of every word, of every step, because with the slightest movement he might provoke the shadow to new action, if anything so grave, so stern, so silent as that Pursuit could be termed action, and . . . it was odd how certainly he knew it . . . so kind. Bunning's face brought him to the sudden necessity of treating the nightmare as reality, for the moment at any rate. The staring spectacles piteously appealed to him—

"I can't stand it—I can't stand it."

"Hush!" Olva held his hand, and out of the fog, below in the Court, a voice was calling—"Craven! Craven! Buck up, you old ass!"

"They're going to light bonfires and things," Bunning quavered, and then, with a hand that had always before seemed soft and flabby but that was now hard and burning, he caught Olva's wrist. "I had to see you—I've been three days now—waiting—all the time for them to come and arrest you. Oh! I've imagined everything—everything—and the fog makes it worse. . . . Oh! my God! I can't stand it."

The man was on the edge of hysteria. His senseless giggle threatened that in another instant it would be beyond all control. There was no time to be lost. Olva took him by the shoulders, held him firmly and looked straight into the weak, quivering eyes that were behind the glasses like fish in a tank.

"Look here, Bunning. Pull yourself together. You must—you must. Do you understand? If you've never done it before you must do it now. Remember that you wanted to help me. Well, now you can do it— but remember that if you give way so that people notice you, then the show's up. They'll be asking questions—they'll watch you—and you'll have done for me. Otherwise there's no risk whatever—no risk whatever. Just remember that—it's as though I'd never done anything; everything's going on in its usual way; life will always be just the same . . . if you'll keep hold of yourself—do you understand? Do you hear me?"

Bunning's quavering voice answered him, "I'll try."

"Well, look here. Think of it quite calmly, naturally. You're taking it like a story that you'd read in a magazine or a play you'd seen at a theatre—melodrama with all the lights on and every one screaming. Well, it can be like that if you want it. Every one thinks of murder that way and you can go shrieking to the Dean and have the rope round my neck in a minute. But I want you to think of it as the most ordinary thing in the world. Remember no one knows but yourself, and they won't know either if you behave in a natural sort of way." Then suddenly his voice sank to a growl and he caught the man's hands in his and held the whole quivering body in his control—"Quiet!" he muttered, "Quiet!"

Bunning had begun to laugh—quite helplessly, almost noiselessly—only his fat cheeks were quivering and his mouth foolishly, weakly smiling: his eyes seemed to be disconnected from his body and to be protesting against it. They looked out like a prisoner from behind barred windows. The body began to shake from head to foot-ripples of noiseless laughter shook his fat limbs, then suddenly he began . . . peal upon peal. . . the tears came rolling down, the mouth was loosely trembling, and still only the eyes, in a kind of sad, stupid wonder, protested.

Olva seized his throat-"Stop it, you damned fool!" . . . He looked straight into the eyes—Bunning ceased as suddenly as he had begun. The horrible, helpless noise fell with a giggle into silence; he collapsed into a chair and hid his face in his hands.

There was a long pause. Olva gazed at the bending figure, summoning all his will power to hold the shaking thing in control. He waited. Then, softly, he began again. "Bunning, I did you a great wrong when I told you—you're not up to it."

From behind the hands there came a muffled voice—"I am up to it."

"This sort of thing makes it impossible."

"It shall never happen again." Bunning lifted his tear-stained face. "It's been coming for days. I've been so dreadfully frightened. But now—that I've been with you—it's better, much better. If only—" and his voice caught—"if only—no one suspects."

Olva gravely answered, "No one suspects."

"If I thought that any one—that there was any chance—that any one had an idea. . . ."

Craven's voice was echoing in Olva's ears. He answered again—

"No one has the slightest suspicion."

Bunning got up heavily from the chair—"I shall be better now. It's been so awful having a secret. I never could keep one. I always used to do wrong things at home and then tell them and then get punished.

But I will try. But if I thought that they guessed—" There was a rap on the door and Bunning gasped, stepped back against the wall, his face white, his knees trembling.

"Don't be such a fool," Olva said fiercely. "If you're like that every time any one knocks you may as well chuck it at once. Look sensible, man. Pull yourself together."

Lawrence entered, bringing log with him from the stairs. His big, thick-set body was so reassuring, so healthy in its sturdiness, so strange a contrast to the trembling figure against the wall that Olva felt an immense relief.

"You know Bunning, Lawrence?"

"How do?"

Lawrence gripped Bunning's fingers, nodded to Bunning's stumbling words and smiled genially.

Bunning got to the door, blinked upon them both from behind his glasses and was gone—muttering something about "work . . . letters to write."

"Rum feller," said Lawrence, and dismissed him with a chuckle. "Shouldn't ever have thought him your style, Dune . . . but you're a clever feller and clever fellers always see more in stupid fellers than ordinary fellers do . . . come out and see the rag."

"Rag! What rag?"

"It's November 5th."

So it was. In the air already perhaps there were those mysterious signs and portents that heralded riot—nothing, as yet, for the casual observer to notice, nothing but a few undergraduates arm-in-arm pacing the sleepy streets—a policeman here, a policeman there. Every now and again clocks strike the quarters, and in many common-rooms heads are nodding over ancient Port and argument of the gentlest kind is being tossed to and fro. But, nevertheless, we remember other Fifths of November. There was that occasion in '98, that other more distant time in '93. . . . There was that furious battle in the Market Place when the Town Hall was nearly set on fire and a policeman had his arm broken.

These are historic occasions; on the other hand the fateful date has passed, often enough, without the merest flinging of a squib or friendly appropriation of the genial policeman's helmet.

No one can say, no one knows, whether there will be riot to-night or no. Most of the young gentlemen now parading the K.P. and Petty Cury would undoubtedly prefer that there should be a riot. For one thing there has been no riot during the last five or six years—no one "up" just now has had any experience of such a thing, and it would be beyond question delightful to taste the excitement of it. But, on the other hand, there is all the difficulty of getting under way. One cannot possibly enjoy the occasion until one has reached that delightful point when one has lost all sense of risk, when recklessly we pile the bonfire, snap our fingers in the nose of poor Mr. Gregg who is terrific enough when he marches solemnly into Chapel but is nothing at all when he is screaming with shrill anger amongst the lights and fury of the blazing common.

Will this wonderful moment when discipline, respect for authority, thoughts of home, terrors of being sent down, all these bogies, are flung derisively to the winds arrive to-night? It has struck nine, and to Olva and Lawrence, walking solemnly through the market-place, it all seems quiet enough.

But behold how the gods work their will! It so happens that Giles of St Martin's has occasion, on this very day, to celebrate his twenty-first birthday. It has been done as a twenty-first birthday should be done, and by nine o'clock the company, twenty in number, have decided that "it was the ruddiest of ruddy old worlds"—that—"let's have some moretodrink ol' man—it was Fifth o' November—and that a ruddyoldbonfire would be—a—ruddyol'-joke—"

Now, at half-past nine, the company of twenty march singing down the K.P. and gather unto themselves others—a murmur is spreading through the byways. "Bonfire on the Common." "Bonfire on the Common." The streets begin to be black with undergraduates.

II

Olva was conscious as he passed with Lawrence through the now crowded streets that Bunning's hysteria had had an effect upon his nerves. He could not define it more directly than by saying that the Shadow that had, during these many weeks, appeared to be pursuing him, at a distance, now seemed to be actually with him. It was as though three of them, and not two, were walking there side by side. It was as though he were himself whispering in his own ear some advice of urgent pleading that he was himself rejecting . . . he was even weighted with the sense of some enlarged growth, of having in fact to carry more, physically as well as spiritually, than he had ever carried before. Now it quite definitely and audibly pleaded—

"Submit—submit—submit. . . . See the tangle that you are getting yourself into. See the trouble that you are getting others into. See the tangle and muddle that you are making of it all. . . . Submit. . . . Give in. . . . You're beaten."

But he was not beaten. Neither the love of Margaret, nor the suspicions of Rupert, nor the hysteria of Bunning had as yet defeated him . . . and even as he resisted it was as though he were fighting himself.

Sidney Street was now quite black with thronging undergraduates moving towards the Common. There was very little noise in it all; every now and again some voice would call aloud to some other voice and would be answered back; a murmur like the swelling of some stream, unlike, in its uniformity and curious evenness of note, any human conversation, seemed to cling to the old grey walls. All of it at present orderly enough but with sinister omen in its very quiet.

Olva felt an increasing excitement as he moved. It was an excitement that had some basis in the stir that was about him, in the murmur like bees of the crowd, in the soft stirring of grey branches above the walls of the street against the night sky, in the golden lights that, set in dim towers, shone high up above their heads. In all these things there was a mysterious tremor that beat, with the rhythm of a pulse, from the town's very heart—but there was more than that in his excitement. There was working in him a conviction that he was now, even now, reaching the very climax of his adventure. Very certainly, very surely, the moment was thawing near, and even in the instant when he had, that very evening, left his rooms, he had stepped, he instinctively knew, out of one stage into another.

"Where are we going?" he asked Lawrence.

"Common. There's goin' to be an old fire. Hope there's a row—don't mind who I hit."

The side streets that led to the Common made progress more difficult, and, with the increased difficulty, came also a more riotous spirit. Some one started "The Two Obadiahs," and it was lustily sung with a good deal of repetition; several people had wooden rattles, intended to encourage College boats during the races, but very useful just now. There were, at the point where the street plunges into the Common, some wooden turnstiles, and these of course were immensely in the way and men were flung about and there was a good deal of coarse pleasantry, and one mild freshman, who had been caught into the crowd by accident, was thrown on to the ground and very nearly trodden to death.

The sight of the vast and mysterious Common put every one into the best of spirits. There was room here to do anything, and it was also dark enough and wide enough to escape if escape were advisable. Moreover the space of it seemed so limitless that it negatived any one's responsibility. A sudden delightful activity swept over the world, and it was immediately every one's business to get wood from anywhere at all and drag it into the middle of the Common. As they moved through the turnstiles Olva fancied that he caught sight of Craven.

On the Common's edge, with bright little lights in their windows, were perched a number of tiny houses with strips of garden in front of them. These little eyes watched, apprehensively no doubt, the shadowy mass that hovered under the night sky. They did not like this kind of thing, these little houses—they remembered five or six years ago when their cabbages had been trampled upon, their palings torn down, even hand-to-hand contests in the passages and one roof on fire. Where were the police? The little eyes watched anxiously. There was no sign of the police. . . .

Olva smiled at himself for the excitement that he was feeling. He was standing at present with Lawrence on the edge of the Common, watching, but he was feeling irresistibly drawn towards the dark pile of wood that was rising slowly towards the sky.

"As though one were ten years old"—and yet there was Lawrence murmuring, "I'd awfully like to hit somebody." And that, after all, was what it all came to. Perhaps Olva, if there were really to be some "scraps," would be able to work off some of his apprehension, of his breathlessness. Oh! for one wild ten minutes when scruples were flung to the winds, when there was at last in front of one an enemy whom one could touch, whom one could fling, physically, brutally, down before one!

"The worst of it is," Lawrence was saying, "there are these town cads—they'll be in the back somewhere shoutin' 'It 'im, 'Varsity,' or somethin' and then runnin' for their lives if they see a Robert comin' . . . it's rotten bein', mixed up with such muck . . . anyhow I'm goin' to have a dash at it—" and he had suddenly plunged forward into space.

Olva was alone. A breeze blew across the Common, the stars twinkled and jumped as though they were suffering from a nervous attack, and with every moment restraint was flung a farther distance, more voices called aloud and shouted, more men poured out of the little side streets. It had the elements of a great mystery. It was as though Mother Earth had, with a heave of her breast, tossed these shadowy forms into the air and was herself stirring with the emotion of their movement.

There was an instant's breathless silence; to the roar of a shouting multitude a bright hard flame shot like steel into the air—the bonfire was alight.

Now with every moment it mounted higher. Black pigmy figures were now dancing round it and across the Common other figures were always passing, dragging wood with them. The row of palings towards the river had gone and soon those little cottages that lined the grass must suffer. Surely now the whole of the University was gathered there! The crowd was close now, dense—men shoved past one another crying out excited cries, waving their arms with strange meaningless gestures. They were arriving rapidly at that condition when they had neither names nor addresses but merely impulses.

Most dangerous element of all threatened that ring of loafers on the outskirts—loafers from the town. Here in this "mob of excited boys" was opportunity for them of getting something back on that authority that had so often treated them with ignominy. . . . Their duty to shout approval, to insult at a distance, to run for their lives were their dirty bodies in any danger . . . but always to fan the flame—"Good old— Varsity—Let them have it, the dirty—" "Pull their shirts off—"

Screams, laughter, shouting, wild dancing—let the Dons come now and see what they can make of it!

"Bulldogs!" sounded a voice in Olva's ear, and turning round he beheld a breathless, dishevelled Bunning. "I've been pulling wood off the palings. Ha! hoch! he! (such noises to recover his breath). Such a rag!"—and then more apprehensively, "Bulldogs! There they are, with Metcher!" They stood, two big men in top-hats, plainly to be seen behind a Don in cap and gown, upon a little hill to the right of the bonfire. The flames lit their figures. Metcher, the Don, was reading something from a paper, and, round the hill, derisively dancing, were many undergraduates. Apparently the Proctor found the situation too difficult for him and presently he disappeared. Bunning watched him, apprehension and a sense of order struggling' with a desire for adventure. "They've gone to fetch the police. There'll be an awful row."

There probably would be because that moment had at last been reached when authority was flung absolutely to the winds of heaven. The world seemed, in a moment, to have gone mad. Take Bunning, his cheeks flushed, his body shaking, his eyes flaming, for an example. Olva, dark, motionless in his shadow, watched it all and waited for his moment. He knew that it was coming. Grimly he addressed the Shadow, now close to his very heart. "I know you. You are urging me on. This night is your business. . . . But I am fighting you still! I am fighting you still!"

The moment came. Bunning, clutching on to Olva's sleeve, whispered, "The police! Even at that crisis of intensest excitement he could be seen, nervously, pushing his spectacles up his nose. A surging crowd of men, and Olva again fancied that he caught sight of Craven, swept towards the row of timid twinkling lights with their neat little gardens like trembling protests laid out before them. More wood! more wood! to appease that great flaming monster that shot tongues of fire now to the very heavens. More wood! more wood!"

"Look out, the police!"

They came, with their truncheons, in a line down the Common. Olva was flung into the heart of a heaving mass of legs and arms. He caught a glimpse of Bunning behind and he thought that he saw Craven a little to his right. He did not know—he did not care. His blood was up at last. He was shouting he knew not what, he was hitting out with his fists. Men's voices about him—"Let go, you beast." "My God, I'll finish you." "There goes a bobby." "Stamp on him!"

A disgraceful scene. The policemen were hopelessly outnumbered. The crowd broke on to the line of orderly little gardens, water was poured from windows, the palings were flung to the ground—glass broken—screams of women somewhere in the distance.

But even now Olva knew that his moment had not come. Then some one shouted in his ear—"Town cads! They're murdering a bobby!" He was caught with several other men (of their number was Bunning) off the Common up a side street.

A blazing lamp showed him an angry, shouting, jeering crowd; figures closed round something on the ground. Four men had joined arms with him, and now the five of them, shouting "'Varsity!" hitting right and left, rushed into the circle. The circle broke and Olva saw lying his length on the ground, half-stunned, clothed only in a torn shirt of bright blue, a stout heavy figure—once obviously, from the clothes flung to one side, a policeman, now with his large red face in a muddy puddle, his fat naked legs bent beneath him, his fingers clutching dirt, nothing very human at all. Town cads of the worst! Some brute now was raising his foot and kicking the bare flesh!

Instantly the world was on flame for Olva. Now again, as once in Sannet Wood, he must hit and hit with all his soul. He broke, like a madman, into the heart of the crowd, sending it flying. There were cries and screams.

He was conscious of three faces. There was Bunning there, white, staring. There was Craven, with his back to a house-door, staring also—and directly before him was a purple face with muddy hair fringing it and little beady eyes. The face of the brute who had been kicking! He must hit. He struck and his fist broke the flesh! He was exultant . . . at last he had, after these weeks of intangibility, found something solid. The face broke away from him. The circle scattered back and the fat, naked body was lying in the mud alone. There was a sudden silence. Olva, conscious of a great power surging through his body, raised his hand again.

A voice, shrill, terror in it, screamed, "Look out, man, he'll kill you!"

He turned and saw under the lamplight Craven, his eyes blazing, his finger pointed. He was suddenly cold from head to foot. The voice came, it had seemed, from heaven. Craven's eyes were alive now with certainty. Then there was another cry from somewhere of "The police!" and the crowd had melted. In the little street now there were only the body of the policeman and a handful of undergraduates.

They raised the man, poured water over him, found some of his clothes, and two men led him, his head lolling, down the street.

There was a noisy world somewhere in the distance, but here there was silence. Olva crept slowly out of his exultation and found himself in the cold windy street with Bunning for his only companion.

Bunning—now a torn, dirty, bleeding Bunning—gripped his arm.

"Did you hear?"

"Hear what?"

"Craven—when you were fighting there—Craven was watching . . . I saw it all . . . Craven suspects."

Olva met the frightened eyes—"He does not suspect."

"Didn't you hear? He called out to the cad you were going for. . . ." Then, in a kind of whimper, dismal enough in the dreary little street—"He'll find out—Craven—I know he will. . . . Oh! my God! what shall I do!"

Some one had broken the glass of the street lamp and the gas flared above them, noisily.

CHAPTER XII

LOVE TO THE "VALSE TRISTE"

I

It was all, when one looked back upon it, the rankest melodrama. The darkness, the flaming lamp, Craven's voice and eyes, Bunning . . . it had all arranged itself as though it bad been worked by a master dramatist. At any rate there they now were, the three of them—Olva, Bunning, Craven—placed in a situation that could not possibly stay as it was. In which direction was it going to develop? Bunning had no control at all, it would be he who would supply the next move . . . meanwhile in the back of Olva's mind there was that banging sense of urgency, no time to be lost. He must see Margaret and speak before Rupert spoke to her. Perhaps, even now, Craven was not certain. If he only knew of how much Craven was sure! Did he feel sure enough to speak to Margaret?

Meanwhile the first and most obvious thing was that Bunning was in a state of terror that threatened instant exposure. The man was evidently realizing that now, for the first time, he had a big thing with which he must grapple. He must grapple with his devotion to Olva, with his terror of Craven, but, most of all, with his terror of himself. That last was obviously the thing that tortured him, for, having now been given by the High Gods an opportunity of great service, so miserable a creature did he consider himself that he would not for an instant trust his control. He was trying, Olva saw, with an effort that in its intensity was pathetic to prove himself worthy of the chance that had been offered him, as though it were the one sole opportunity that he would ever be given, but to appear to the world something that he was not was an art that Bunning and his kind could never acquire—that is their tragedy. It was the fate of Bunning that his boots and spectacles should always negative any attempt that he might make at a striking personality.

On the night after the "Rag" he sat in Olva's room and made a supreme effort at control.

"If you can only hold on," Olva told him, "to the end of term. It's only a week or two now. Just stick it until then; you won't be bothered with me after that."

"You're going away?"

"I don't know—it depends."

"I don't know what I should do if you went. To have to stand that awful secret all alone . . . only me knowing. Oh! I couldn't! I couldn't! and now that Craven—"

"Craven knows nothing. He doesn't even suspect anything. See here, Bunning"—Olva crossed over to him and put his hand on his shoulder. "Can't you understand that your behaviour makes me wish that I hadn't told you, whereas if you care as you say you do you ought to want to show me how you can carry it, to prove to me that I was right to tell you—"

"Yes, I know. But Craven—"

"Craven knows nothing."

"But he does." Bunning's voice became shrill and his fat hand shook on Olva's arm. "There's something I haven't told you. This morning in Outer Court he stopped me."

"Craven stopped you?"

"Yes. There was no one about. I was going along to my rooms and he met me and he said: 'Hullo, Bunning.'"

"Well?"

"I'd been thinking of it—of his knowing, I mean—all night, so I was dreadfully startled, dreadfully startled. I'm afraid I showed it."

"Get on. What did he say?"

"He said: 'Hullo, Bunning!'"

"Yes, you've told me that. What else?"

"I said 'Hullo!' I was dreadfully startled. I don't think he'd ever spoken to me before. And then he looked so strange—wild, as though he hadn't slept, and white, and his eyes moved all the time. I'm afraid he saw that I was startled."

"Do get on. What else did he ask you?"

"He asked me whether I'd enjoyed last night. He said: 'You were with Dune, weren't you?' He cried, as though he wasn't speaking to me at all: 'That's an odd sort of friend for you to have.' I ought to have been angry I suppose, but I was shaking all over . . . yes . . . well . . . then he said: 'I thought you were in with all those pi men,' and I just couldn't say anything at all—I was shaking so. He must have thought I looked very odd."

"I'm sure he did," said Olva drily. "Well it won't be many days before you give the show away—that's certain."

What could have made him tell the fellow? What madness? What—?

But Bunning caught on to his sleeve.

"No, no, you mustn't say that, Dune, please, you mustn't. I'm going to do my best, I am really. But his coming suddenly like that, just when I'd been thinking. . . . But it's awful. I told you if any one suspected it would make it so hard—"

"Look here, Bunning, perhaps it will help you if you know the way that I'm feeling about it. I'll try and explain. All these days there's something in me that's urging me to go out and confess."

"Conscience," said Bunning solemnly.

"No, it isn't conscience at all. It's something quite different, because the thing that's urging me isn't urging me because I've done something I'm ashamed of, it's urging me because I'm in a false position. There's that on the one side, and, on the other, I'm in love with Rupert Craven's sister."

Bunning gave a little cry.

"Yes. That complicates things, doesn't it? Now you see why Rupert Craven is the last person who must know anything about it; it's because he loves his sister so much and suspects, I think, that I care for her, that he's going to find out the truth."

"Does she care for you?" Bunning brought out huskily.

"I don't know. That's what I've got to find out."

"Because it all depends on that. If she cares enough it won't matter what you've done, and if she doesn't care enough it won't matter her knowing because you oughtn't to marry her. Oh," and Bunning's eyes as they gazed at Olva were those, once more, of a devoted dog: "she's lucky." Then he repeated, as though to himself, in his odd husky whisper: "Anything that I can do . . . anything that I can do . . ."

II

On the next evening, about five o'clock, Olva went to the house in Rocket Road. He went through a world that, in its frosty stillness, held beauty in its hands like a china cup, so fragile in its colours, so gentle in its outline, with a moon, round and of a creamy white, with a sky faintly red, and stiff trees, black and sharp.

Cambridge came to Olva then as a very lovely thing. The Cambridge life was a lovely thing with its kindness, its simplicity, its optimism. He was penetrated too with a great sadness because he knew that life of that kind was gone, once and for ever, from him; whatever came to him now it could never again be that peace; the long houses flung black shadows across the white road and God kept him company. . . .

Miss Margaret Craven had not yet come in, but would Mr. Dune, perhaps, go up and see Mrs. Craven? The old woman's teeth chattered in the cold little hall. "We are dead, all of us dead here," the skins on the walls seemed to say; "and you'll be dead soon . . . oh! yes, you will."

Olva went up to Mrs. Craven. The windows of her room were tightly closed and a great fire was blazing; before this she lay stretched out on a sofa of faded green—her black dress, her motionless white hands, her pale face, her moving eyes.

She had beside her to-day a little plate of dry biscuits, and, now and again, her hand would move across her black dress and break one of these with a sharp sound, and then her hand would fall back again.

"I am very glad to see you. Draw your chair to the fire. It is a chill day, but fine, I believe."

She regarded him gravely.

"It is not much of life that I can watch from this room, Mr. Dune. It is good of you to come and see me . . . there must be many other things for you to do."

He came at once to the point.

"I want your permission to ask your daughter to marry me, Mrs. Craven."

There was a long silence between them. He seemed, in his inner consciousness, to be carrying on a dialogue.

"You see," he said to the Shadow, "I have forestalled you. I shall ask Margaret Craven this evening to marry me. You cannot prevent that . . . you cannot."

And a voice answered: "All things betray Thee Who betrayest Me."

"You have known us a very short time, Mr. Dune." Mrs. Craven's voice came to him from a great distance.

He felt as though he were speaking to two persons. "Time has nothing to do with falling in love, Mrs. Craven."

He saw to his intense amazement that she was greatly moved. She, who had always seemed to him a mask, now was suddenly revealed as suffering, tortured, intensely human. Her thin white hands were pressed together.

"I am a lonely, unhappy woman, Mr. Dune. Margaret is now all that is left to me. Everything has been taken from me. Rupert—" Her voice was lost; very slowly tears rolled down her cheeks. She began again desperately. "Margaret is all that I have got. If I were left alone it would be too much for me. I could not endure the silence."

It was the more moving in that it followed such stern reserve. His own isolation, the curious sense that he had that they were, both of them, needing protection against the same power (it seemed to him that if he raised his eyes he would see, on the opposite wall, the shadow of that third Presence); this filled him with the tenderest pity, so that suddenly he bent down and kissed her hand.

She caught his with a fierce convulsive movement, and so they sat in silence whilst he felt the pulse of her hand beat through his body, and once a tear rolled from her cheek on to his wrist.

"You understand . . ." she said at last. "You understand. I have always seen that you know. . ." Then she whispered, "How did you know?"

"Know?" He was bewildered, but before she could speak again the door opened and Margaret Craven came in.

She moved with that restrained emotion that he had seen in her when he had first met her. She was some great force held in check, some fire that blazed but must be hidden from the world, and as she bent over her mother and kissed her the embrace had in it something of passionate protest; both women seemed to assert in it their right to quite another sort of life.

He saw that his moment with Mrs. Craven had passed. That fire, that humanity had gone from her and she lay back now on her sofa with the faint waxen lids closed upon her eyes, her hands thinly folded, almost a dead woman.

Margaret kissed her again—now softly and gently, and Olva went with her from the room.

III

He was prepared to find that Rupert had told her everything. He thought that he saw in the gravity and sadness of her manner, and also in the silence that she seemed deliberately at first to place between them, that she was waiting for the right moment to break it to him. He felt that she would ask him gravely and with great kindness, but that, in the answer that he would give her, it must be all over . . . the end. The pursuit would be concluded.

Then suddenly in the way that she looked at him he knew that she had been told nothing.

"I'm afraid that mother is very unwell. I'm afraid that you must have found her so."

"If she could get away—" he began.

"Ah! if we could all get away! If only we could! But we have talked of that before. It is quite impossible. And, even if we could (and how glad I should be!), I do not know that it would help mother. It is Rupert that is breaking her heart!"

"Rupert!"

For answer to his exclamation she cried to him with all the pent-up suffering and loneliness of the last weeks in her voice—

"Ah, Mr. Dune, help me! I shall go mad if something doesn't happen; every day it is worse and I can't grapple with it. I'm not up to it. If only they'd speak out! but it's this silence!" She seemed to pull herself together and went on more quietly: "You know that Rupert and I have been everything to one another all our lives. We have never had a secret of any kind. Until this last month Rupert was the most open, dearest boy in the world. His tenderness with my mother was a most wonderful thing, and to me!—I cannot tell you what he was to me. I suppose, for the very reason that we were so much to one another, we did not make any other very close friends. I had girls in Dresden, of course, and there were men at school and college for whom he cared, but I think there can have been few brothers and sisters who were so entirely together in every way. A month ago that all ceased."

She flung her head back with a sharp defiant movement as though the memory of it hurt her.

"I've told you this before. I talked to you about it when you were here last. But since then he has become much worse and I am afraid that anything may happen. I have no one to go to. It is killing my mother, and then—you were a friend of his."

"I hope that I am now."

"That is the horrible part of it. But it seems now that all this agitation, this trouble, is directed against you."

"Against me"

"Yes, the other evening he spoke about you—here—furiously. He said you must never come here again, that I must never speak to you again. He said that you had done dreadful things. And then when I asked him he could not tell me anything. He seemed—and you must look on it in that light, Mr. Dune—as though he were not in the least responsible for what he said. I'm afraid he is very, very ill. He is dreadfully unhappy, and yet he can explain nothing. I too have been very unhappy, and mother, because we love him."

"If he wishes that I should not come here again—" Olva began.

"But he is not responsible. He really does not know what he is doing. He never had the smallest trouble that he did not confide it to me, and now—"

"I have noticed, of course," Olva said "that lately his manner to me has been strange. I would have helped him if he would let me, but he will not. He will have nothing to say to me . . . I too have been very sorry about it. I have been sorry because I am fond of Rupert, but also—there is another, stronger reason—because I love you, Margaret."

As he spoke he got up and stood by her chair. He saw her take in his last words, at first with a wondering gravity, then with a sudden splendour so that light flooded her face; her arms made a little helpless gesture, and she caught his hand.

He drew her up to him out of her chair; then, with a fierce passionate movement, they held one another and clung together as though in a desperate wild protest against the world.

"You can't touch me now—I've got her," he seemed to fling at the blank face of the old mirror.

It was his act of defiance, but through his exultation he caught the whisper—it might again have been conveyed to him through the shrill shivering notes of the "Valse Triste"—"Tell her—tell her—now. Trust her. Dear son, trust Me . . . it must be so in the end."

"Now," he heard her say, "I can stand it all."

"When you came into this room weeks ago," she went on, "I loved you; from the very first instant. Now I do not mind what any one can do."

"I too loved you from the first instant."

"You were so grave. I tried at first not to think of you as a person at all because I thought that it was safer, and then gradually, although I fought against you, I could not keep you out. You drove your way in. You understood so wonderfully the things that I wanted you to understand. Then Rupert and mother drove me to want you more and more. I thought that you liked me, but I didn't know. . . ." Then with a little shiver she clung to him, pressing close to him. "Oh! hold me, hold me safe."

The room was now gathering to itself that dusk that gave it its strangest air. The fire had fallen low and only shone now in the recesses of the high fireplace with a dull glimmer. Amongst the shadows it seemed that the Presence was gravely waiting. As Olva held Margaret in his arms he felt that he was fighting to keep her.

In the dark hollow of the mirror he thought that he saw the long white road, the mists, the little wood and some one running. . . .

It seemed to him that Margaret was not there, that the room was dark and very heavy, that some bell was ringing in his ear. . . . Then about him a thousand voices were murmuring: "Tell her—tell her—tell her the truth."

With a last effort he tried to cry "I will not tell her."

His lips broke on her name "Margaret." Then, with a little sigh, tumbling forward, he fainted.

CHAPTER XIII

MRS. CRAVEN

I

Afterwards, lying in his easy chair before his fire, he was allowed a brief and beautiful respite. It was almost as though he were already dead—as though, consciously, he might lie there, apart from the world, freed from the eternal pursuit, at last unharassed, and hold, with both hands, that glorious certainty—Margaret.

He had a picture of her now. He was lying where he had tumbled, there on the floor with the silver trays and boxes, the odd tables, the gimcrack chairs all about him. Slowly he had opened his eyes and had gazed, instantly, as though the gates of heaven had rolled back for him, into her face. She was kneeling on the floor, one hand was behind his head, the other bathed his forehead. He could see her breasts (so little, so gentle) rise and fall beneath her thin dress, and her great dark eyes caught his soul and held it.

In that one great moment God withdrew. For the first time in his knowledge of her they were alone, and in the kiss that he gave to her when he drew her down to him they met for the first time. Death and the anger of God might come to him—that great moment could never be taken from him. It was his. . . .

He had seen that she was gravely distressed with his fainting, and he had been able to give her no reason beyond the heat of the room. He could see that she was puzzled and felt that there was some mystery there that she was not to know, but she too had found in that last kiss a glorious certainty that no other hazard could possibly destroy.

He loved her—she loved him. Let the Gods thunder!

But he knew, nevertheless, as he lay back there in the chair, that he had received a sign. That primrose path with Margaret was not to be allowed him, and so sure was he that now he could lie back and look at it all as though he were a spectator and wonder in what way God intended to work it out. The other side of him—the fighting, battling creature—was, for the moment, dormant. Soon Bunning would come in and then the fight would begin again, but for the instant there was peace—the first peace that he had known since that far-away evening in St. Martin's Chapel.

As with a drowning man (it is said) so now with Olva his past life stretched, in panorama, before him. He saw the high rocky grey building with its rough shape and shaggy lichen, its neglected courtyard, its iron-barred windows, the gaunt trees, like witches, that hemmed it, the white ribbon of road, far, far below it, the shining gleam of the river hidden by purple hills. He saw his father—huge, flowing grey beard, eyebrows stuck, like leeches, on to his weather-beaten face, his gnarled and knotted hands. He saw himself a tiny boy with thin black hair and grave eyes watching his father as he bathed in the mill-pool below the house—his father rising naked from the stream, hung with the mists of early morning, naked with enormous chest, huge flanks, his beard black then and sweeping across his breast, his great thighs shining with the dripping water—primitive, primeval, in the heart of the early morning silence.

Many, many other pictures of those first days, but always Olva and his father, moving together, speaking but seldom, sitting before the fire in the evenings, watching the blaze, despising the world. The contempt that his father had for his fellow-beings! Had a man ever been so alone? Olva himself had drunk of that same contempt and welcomed his solitude at Harrow. The world had been with him a place of war, of hostility, until he had struck that blow in Sannet Wood. He remembered the eagerness with which, at the end of term, he had hastened back to his father. After the noise and clatter of school life how wonderful to go back to the still sound of dripping water, to the crackle of dry leaves under foot, to the heavy solemn tread of cattle, to those evenings when at his father's side he heard the coals click in the fire and the old clock on the stairs wheeze out the passing minutes. That relationship with his father bad been, until this term, the only emotion in his life—and now? And now!

It was incredible this change that had come to him. First there was Margaret and then, after her, Mrs. Craven, Rupert, Lawrence, Cardillac, Bunning. All these persons, in varying degree, bad become of concern to him. The world that had always been a place of smoke, of wind, of sky, was now, of a sudden, crowded with figures. He bad been swept from the hill-top down into the market-place. He had been given perhaps one keen glance of a moving world before he was drawn from it altogether. . . . Now, just as he had tasted human companionship and loved it, must he die?

He knew, too, that his recent popularity in the College had pleased him. He wanted them to like him . . . he was proud to feel that because he was he therefore Cardillac resigned, willingly, his place to him. But if Cardillac knew him for a felon, knew that he might be hanged in the dark and flung into a nameless grave, what then? If Cardillac knew what Rupert Craven almost knew, would not his horror be the same? The world, did it only know. . . .

To-morrow was the day of the Dublin match. Olva and Cardillac were both playing, and at the end of the game choice might be made between them. Did Olva care? He did not know . . . but Margaret was coming, and, in the back of his mind, he wanted to show her what he could do.

And yet, whilst that Shadow hovered in the Outer Court, how little a thing this stir and movement was! No tumult that the material world could ever make could sound like that whisper that was with him now again in the room—with him at his very heart—"All things betray Thee. . . ."

The respite was over. Bunning came in.

Change had seized Bunning. Here now was the result of his having pulled himself together. Olva could see that the man bad made up his mind to something, and that, further, he was resolved to keep his purpose secret. It was probably the first occasion in Bunning's life of such resolution. There was a faint colour in the fat cheeks, the eyes bad a little light and the man scarcely spoke at all lest this purpose should trickle from his careless lips. Also as he looked at Olva his customary devotion was heightened by an air of frightened pride.

Olva, watching him, was apprehensive—the devotion of a fool is the most dangerous thing in creation.

"Well, have you seen Craven again?"

"Yes. We had a talk."

"What did he say?"

"Oh, nothing."

"Rot. He didn't stop and talk to you about the weather. Come on, Bunning, what have you been up to?"

"I haven't been up to anything."

The man's lips were closed. For another half an hour Bunning sat in a chair before the fire—silent. Every now and again he flung a glance at Olva. Sometimes he jerked his head towards the window as though he heard a step.

He had the look of a Christian going into the amphitheatre to face the Beasts.

II

About eleven o'clock of the next morning Olva went to see Margaret. He had written to her the night before and asked her not to tell Rupert the news of their engagement immediately, but, when the morning came, he could not rest with that. He must know more.

It was a damp, misty morning, the fine frost had gone. He was going to Margaret to try and recover some reality out of the state that he was in. The recent incidents—Craven's suspicions, the 5th of November evening, Bunning's alarm, the scene with Margaret—bad dragged him for a time from that conviction that he was living in an unreal world. That day when he had run in the snowstorm from Sannet Wood had seemed to him, during these last weeks, absurd and an effect, obviously, of excited nerves. Now, on this morning of the Dublin match, he awoke again to that unreal condition. The bedmaker, the men passing through the Court beneath his windows, the porter at the gate—these people were unreal, and above him, around him, the mist seemed ever about to break into new terrible presences.

"This thing is wearing me down. I shall go off my head if something definite doesn't happen"—and then, there in his room with the stupid breakfast things still on the table, the consciousness of the presence of God seized him so that he felt as though the pursuit were suddenly at an end and there was nothing left now but complete submission.

In this world of wraiths, God was the most certain Presence. . . .

There remained only Margaret. Perhaps she could recover reality for him. He went to her.

He found her waiting for him in the little drawing-room and he could not see her. He knew then that the Pursuing Shadow had taken a new step. It was literally physically true. The room was there, the shining things, the knick-knacks, the mirror, the scent of oranges. He could see her body, her black dress, her eyes, her white neck, the movement towards him that she made when she saw him coming, but there was nothing there. It was as though he had been asked to love a picture.

He could not think of her at all as Margaret Craven or of himself as Olva Dune. Only in the glass's reflection he saw the white road stretching to the wood.

"I really am going off my head. She'll see that something's up"—and then from the bottom of his heart, far away as though it had been the cry of another person, "Oh! how I want her How I want her!"

He took her in his arms and kissed her and felt as though he were dead and she were dead and that they were both, being so young am eager for life, struggling to get back existence again.

Her voice came to him from a long distance "Olva, how ill you look! What is it? What won't you tell me? There's something the matter with you all and you all keep me in the dark."

He said nothing and she went on very gently, "It would be so much better, dear, if you were to tell me. After all, I'm part of you now, aren't I? Perhaps I can help you."

His own voice, from a long distance, said: "I don't think that you can help me, Margaret."

She put her hand on his arm and looked up into his face. "I am trying to help you all, but it is so difficult if you will tell me nothing. And, Olva dear, if it is something that you have done—something that you are afraid to tell me—believe me, dear, that there's nothing—nothing in the world—that you could have done that would matter to me now. I love you—nothing can alter that."

He tried to feel that the hand on his arm was real. With a great effort he spoke: "Have you told Rupert?"

"Mother told him last night."

"What did he say?"

"I don't know—but they had a terrible scene. Rupert," her lip quivered, "went away without a word last night. Only he told mother that if I would not give you up he would never come into the house again. But he loves me more than any one in the world, and he can't do without me. I know that he can't, and I know that he will come back. Mother wants to see you; perhaps you will go up to her."

She had moved back from him and was looking at him with sad perplexity. He knew that he must seem strange and cold standing there, in the middle of the room, without making any movement towards her, but he could not help himself, he seemed to have no power over his own actions.

Coming up to him she flung her arms round his neck. "Olva, Olva, tell me, I can't endure it"—but slowly he detached himself from her and left her.

As he went through the dark close passage he wondered how God could be so cruel.

When he came into Mrs. Craven's room he knew that her presence comforted him. The dark figure on the faded sofa by the fire seemed to him now more real than anything else in the world. Although Mrs. Craven made no movement yet he felt that she encouraged him come to her, that she wanted him. The room was very dark and bare, and although a large fire blazed in the hearth, it was cold. Beyond the window a misty world, dank, with dripping trees, stretched to a dim horizon. Mrs. Craven did not turn her eyes from the fire when she heard him enter. He felt as though she were watching him and knew that he had drawn a chair beside the sofa. Suddenly she moved her hand towards him and he took it and held it for a moment.

She turned and he saw that she had been crying.

"I had a talk with my son last night," she said at last, and her voice seemed to him the saddest thing that he had ever heard. "We had always loved one another until lately. Last night he spoke to me as he has never spoken before. He was very angry and I know that he did not mean all that he said to me—but it hurt me."

"I'm afraid, Mrs. Craven, that it was because of me. Rupert is very angry with me and he refuses to consent to Margaret's marriage with me. Is not that so?"

"Yes, but it is not only that. For many weeks now he has not been himself with me. I am not a happy woman. I have had much to make me unhappy. My children are a very great deal to me. I think that this has broken my heart."

"Mrs. Craven, if there is anything that I can do that will put things right, if I can say anything to Rupert, if I can tell him anything, explain anything, I will. I think I can tell you, Mrs. Craven, why it is that Rupert does not wish me to marry Margaret. I have something to confess—to you."

Then he was defeated at last? He had surrendered? In another moment the words "I killed Carfax and Rupert knows that I killed him" would have left his lips—but Mrs. Craven had not heard his words. Her face was turned away from him again and she spoke in a strange, monotonous voice as one speaks in a dream.

The words seemed to be created out of the faded sofa, the misty window, the dim shadowy bed. She was crying—her hands were pressed to her face—the words came between her sobs.

"It is too much for me. All these years I have kept silence. Now I can bear it no longer. If Rupert leaves me, it will kill me, but unless I speak to some one I shall die of all this silence, . . . I cannot bear any longer to be alone with God."

Was it his own voice? Were these his own words? Had things gone so far with him that he did not know—"I cannot bear any longer to be alone with God. . . ." Was not that his own perpetual cry?

"Mr. Dune, I killed my husband."

In the silence that followed the only sound was her stifled crying and the crackling fire.

"You knew from the beginning."

"No, I did not know."

"But you were different from all the others. I felt it at once when I saw you. You knew, you understood, you were sorry for me."

"I am sorry. I understand. But I did not know."

"Let me tell you." She turned her face towards him and began to speak eagerly.

He took her hand between his.

"Oh! the relief—now at once—after all these years of silence. Fifteen years. . . . It happened when Rupert was a tiny boy. You see he was a bad man. I found it out almost at once—after a month or two. But I loved him madly—utterly. I did not care about his being bad—that does not matter to a woman—but he set about breaking my heart. It amused him. Margaret was born. He used to terrify me with the things that he would teach her. He said that he would make her as big a devil as he was himself. I prayed God that I might never have another child and then Rupert was born. From that moment my one prayer was that my husband might die.

"At last my opportunity came. He fell ill—dreadful attacks of heart—and one night he had a terrible attack and I held back the medicine that would have saved him. I saw his eyes watching me, pleading for it. I stood and waited . . . he died."

She stopped for a moment—then her words came more slowly: "It was a very little thing—it was not a very bad thing—he was a wicked man . . . but God has punished me and He will punish me until I die. All these years He has pursued me, urging me to confess—I have fought and struggled against it, but at last He has beaten me—He has driven me. . . . Oh! the relief! the relief!"

She looked at him curiously.

"If you did not know, why did I feel that you understood and sympathized? Have you no horror of me now?"

For answer, he bent and kissed her cheek.

"I too am very lonely. I too know what God can do."

Then she clung to him as though she would never let him leave her.

CHAPTER XIV

GOD

I

Half an hour later he was in his room again, and the real world had come back to him. It had come back with the surprise of some supernatural mechanism; it was as though the sofa, chairs, pictures had five minutes before been grass and toadstools in a world of mist and now were sofa, chairs and pictures again.

He was absolutely sane, whereas half an hour ago he had been held almost by an enchantment. If Margaret were here with him now, here in his room—not in that dim, horrible Rocket Road house, raised it might almost seem by the superstitions and mists of his own conscience—ah! how he would love her!

He was filled with a sense of energy and enterprise. He would have it out with Rupert, laugh away his suspicions, reconcile him to the idea of the marriage, finally drag Margaret from that horrible house. As with a man who has furious attacks of neuralgia, and between the agony of them feels, so great is the relief, that no pain will ever come to him again, so Olva was now, for an instant, the Olva of a month ago.

Four times had the Pursuer thus given him respite—on the morning after the murder, in St. Martin's Chapel on that same evening, after his confession to Bunning, and now. But Aegidius, looking down from his wall, saw the strong, stern face of his young friend and loved him and knew that, at last, the pursuit was at an end. . . .

Bunning came in.

II

Bunning came in. The little silver clock had just struck a quarter to one. The match was at half-past two.

Olva knew at his first sight of Bunning that something had happened. The man seemed dazed, he dragged his great legs slowly after him and planted them on the floor as though he wanted something that was secure, like a man who had begun desperately to slip down a crevasse. His back was bowed and his cheeks were flushed as though some one had been striking him, but his eyes told Olva everything. They were the eyes of a child who has been wakened out of sleep and sees Terror.

"What is it? Sit down. Pull yourself together."

"Oh! Dune! . . . My God, Dune!" The man's voice had the unreality of men walking in a cinematograph. "Craven's coming."

"Coming! Where?"

"Here!"

"Now?"

"I don't know—when. He knows."

"You told him?"

"I thought it best. I thought I was doing right. It's all gone wrong. Oh! these last two days! what I've suffered!"

Now for the first time in the history of the whole affair Olva Dune may be said to have felt sheer physical terror, not terror of the mist, of the road, of the darkness, of the night, but terror of physical things—of the loss of light and air, of the denial of food, of physical death. . . . For a moment the room swam about him. He heard, in the Court below him, some men laughing—a dog was barking. Then he saw that Bunning was on the edge of hysteria. The bedmaker would come in and find him laughing—as he had laughed once before.

Olva stilled the room with a tremendous effort—the floor sank, the table and chairs tossed no longer.

"Now, Bunning, tell me quickly. They'll be here to lay lunch in a minute. What have you told Craven? And why have you told him anything?"

"I told him—yesterday—that I did it."

"That you did it?"

"Yes, that I murdered Carfax."

"My God! You fool! . . . You fool!"

A most dangerous thing this devotion of a fool.

But, strangely, Olva's words roused in Bunning a kind of protest, so that he pulled his eyes back into their sockets, steadied his hands, held his boots firmly to the floor, and, quite softly, with a little note of urgency in it as though he were pleading before a great court, said—

"Yes, I know. But he drove me to it; Craven did. I thought it was the only way to save you. He's been at me now for days; ever since that time he stopped me in Outer Court and asked me why I was a friend of yours. He's been coming to my room—at night—at all sorts of times—and just sitting there and looking at me."

Olva came across and touched Bunning's arm: "Poor Bunning! What a brute I was to tell you!"

"He used to come and say nothing—just look at me. I couldn't stand it, you know. I'm not a clever man—not at all clever—and I used to try and think of things to talk about, but it always seemed to come back to Carfax—every time."

"And then—when you told me the other day about your caring for Miss Craven—I felt that I must do something. I'd always puzzled, you know, why I should be brought into it at all. I didn't seem to be the sort of fellow who'd be likely to be mixed up with a man like you. I felt that it must be with some purpose, you know, and now—now—I thought I suddenly saw—

"I don't know—I thought he'd believe me—I thought he'd tell the police and they'd arrest me—and that'd be the end of it."

Here Bunning took a handkerchief and began miserably to gulp and sniff.

"But, good heavens!" Olva cried, "you didn't suppose that they wouldn't discover it all at the police-station in a minute! Two questions and you'd be done! Why, man—!"

"I didn't know. I thought it would be all right. I was all alone that afternoon, out for a walk by myself—and you'd told me how you did it. I'd only got to tell the same story. I couldn't see how any one should know—I couldn't really . . . I don't suppose"—many gulps—"that I thought much about that—I only wanted to save you."

How bright and wonderful the day! How full of colour the world! And it was all over, all absolutely, finally done.

"Now—look here, stop that sniffing—it's all right. I'm not angry with you. Just tell me exactly what you said to Craven yesterday when you told him."

Bunning thought. "Well, he came into my room quite early after my breakfast. I was reading my Bible, as I used to, you know, every morning, to see whether I could be interested again, as I used to be. I was finding I couldn't when Craven came in. He looked queer. He's been looking queerer every day, and I don't think he's been sleeping. Then he began to ask me questions, not actually about anything, but odd questions like, Where was I born? and Why did I read the Bible? and things like that—just to make me comfortable—and his eyes were so funny, red and small and never still. Then he got to you."

The misery now in Bunning's eyes was more than Olva could bear. It was dumb, uncomprehending misery, the unhappiness of something caught in a trap—and that trap this glittering dancing world!

"Then he got to you! He always asked me the same questions. How long I'd known you?—Why we got on together when we were so different?—silly meaningless things—and he didn't listen to my answers. He was always thinking of the next things to ask and that frightened me so."

The misery in Bunning's eyes grew deeper.

"Suddenly I thought I saw what was meant—that I was intended to take it on myself. It made me warm all over, the though of it. . . . Now, I was going to do something . . . that's how I saw it!"

"Going to do something . . ." he repeated desperately, with choking sobs between the words. "It's all happened so quickly. He had just said absently, not looking at me, 'You like Dune, don't you?'

"When I came out with it all at once—I said, 'Yes, I know, I know what you want. You think that Dune killed Carfax and that I know he did, but he didn't I killed Carfax. . . .'"

Bunning's voice quite rang out. His eyes now desperately sought Olva's face, as though he would find there something that would make the world less black.

"I wasn't frightened—not then—that was the odd thing. The only thing I thought about was saving you—getting you out of it. I didn't see! I didn't see!"

"And then—what did Craven say?" Olva asked quietly.

"Craven said scarcely anything. He asked me whether I realized what I was saying, whether I saw what I was in for? I said 'Yes'—that it had all been too much for my conscience, that I had to tell some one—all the things that you told me. Then he asked me why I'd done it. I told him because Carfax always bullied me—he did, you know—and that one day I couldn't stand it any longer and I met him in the wood and hit him. He said, 'You must be very strong,' and of course I'm not, you know, and that ought to have made me suspect something. But it didn't. . . . Then he said he must think over what he ought to do, but all the time he was saying it I knew he was thinking of something else and then he went away."

"That was yesterday morning?"

"Yesterday morning, and all day I was terrified, but happy too. I thought I'd done a big thing and I thought that the police would come and carry me off. . . . Nothing happened all day. I sat there waiting. And I thought of you—that you'd be able to marry Miss Craven and would be very happy.

"Then, this morning, coming from chapel, Craven stopped me. I thought he was going to tell me that he'd thought it his duty to give me away. He would, you know. But it wasn't that.

"All he said was: 'I wonder how you know so much about it, Bunning.' I couldn't say anything. Then he said, 'I'm going to ask Dune.' That was all . . . all," he wretchedly repeated, and then, with a movement of utter despair, flung his head into his hands, and cried.

Olva, standing straight with his hands at his side, looked through his window at the world—at the white lights on the lower sky, at the pearl grey roofs and the little cutting of dim white street and the high grey college wall. He was to begin again, it seemed, at the state in which he'd been on the day after Carfax's murder. Then he had been sure that arrest would only be a question of hours and he had resolutely faced it with the resolve that he would drain all the life, all the vigour, all the fun from the minutes that remained to him.

Now he had come back to that. Craven would give him away, perhaps . . . he would, at any rate, drive him away from Margaret. But he would almost certainly feel it his duty to expose him. He would feel that that would end the complication with his sister once and for all—the easiest way. He would feel it his duty—these people and their duty!

Well, at least he would have his game of football first—no one could take his afternoon away from him. Margaret would be there to watch him and he would play! Oh! he would play as he had never played in his life before!

Bunning's voice came to him from a great distance—

"What are you going to do? What are you going to say to Craven?"

"Say to him? Why, I shall tell him, of course—tell him everything."

Bunning leapt from his chair. In his urgency he put his hands on Olva's arm: "No, no, no. You mustn't do that. Why it will be as though I'd murdered you. Tell him I did it. Make him believe it. You can—you're clever enough. Make him feel that I did it. You mustn't, mustn't—let him know. Oh, please, please. I'll kill myself if you do. I will really."

Olva gravely, quietly, put his hands on Bunning's shoulders.

"It's all right—it had to come out. I've been avoiding it all this time, escaping it, but it had to come. Don't you be afraid of it. I daresay Craven won't do anything. After all he loves his sister and she cares for him. That will influence him. But, anyhow, all that's done with. There are bigger things in question than Craven knowing about Carfax, and you were meant to tell him—you were really. You've just forced me to see what's the right thing to do—that's all."

Bunning was, surely, in the light of it, a romantic figure.

Miss Annett came in with the lunch.

III

As Olva was changing into his football things, Cardillac appeared.

"Come up to the field with me, will you? I've got a hansom."

Olva finished tying his boots and stood up. Cardillac looked at him.

"My word, you seem fit."

"Yes, I'm splendid, thanks."

He felt splendid. Never before had he been so conscious of the right to be alive. His football clothes smelt of the earth and the air. He moved his arms and legs with wonderful freedom. His blood was pumping through his body as though death, disease, infirmity such things—were of another planet.

For such a man as he there should only be air, love, motion, the begetting of children, the surprising splendour of a sudden death. Now already Craven was waiting for him.

He had sent a note round to Craven's rooms; he had said, "Come in to see me after the match—five o'clock. I have something to tell you."

At five o'clock then. . . .

Meanwhile it was nice of Cardillac to come. They exchanged no words about it, but they understood one another entirely. It was as though Cardillac had said—"I expect that you're going to knock me out of this Rugger Blue as you knocked me out of the Wolves, and I want to show you that we're pals all the way through."

What Cardillac really said was—"Have a cigarette? These are Turkish. Feel like playing a game to-day?"

"Never felt better in my life."

"Well, these Dublin fellows haven't had their line crossed yet this season. May one of us have the luck to do it."

"Pretty hefty lot of forwards."

"Yes, O'Brien's their spot Three I believe."

Olva and Cardillac attracted much attention as they walked through the College. Miss Annett, watching them from a little window where she washed plates, gulped in her thin throat with pride for "that Mr. Dune. There's a gentleman!" The sun above the high grey buildings broke slowly through yellow clouds. The roads were covered with a thin fine mud and, from the earth, faint clouds of mist rose and vanished into a sky that was slowly crumbling from thick grey into light watery blue.

The cold air beat upon their faces as the hansom rattled past Dunstan's, over the bridge, and up the hill towards the field.

Cardillac talked. "There goes Braff. He doesn't often come up to a game nowadays—must be getting on for seventy—the greatest half the 'Varsity's ever had, I suppose."

"It's a good thing this mud isn't thicker. It won't make the ball bad. That game against Monkstown the other day! My word. . . ."

But Olva was not listening. It seemed to him now that two separate personalities were divided in him so sharply that it was impossible to reconcile them.

There was Olva Dune concentrating all his will, his mentality, upon the game that he was about to play. This was his afternoon. After it there would be darkness, death, what you will—parting from Margaret— all purely physical emotions.

The other Olva felt nothing physical. The game, confession to Rupert, trial, imprisonment, even separation from Margaret, all these things were nothing in comparison with some great business that was in progress behind it all, as real life may go on behind the painted back cloth of a stage. Here were amazing happenings, although at present he was confused and bewildered by them. It was not that Olva was, actually, at the instant conscious of actual impressions, but rather that great emotions, great surprising happiness, seemed to shine on some horizon. It was as though something had said to his soul, "Presently you will feel a joy, a splendour, that you had never in your wildest thoughts imagined."

The pursuit was almost at an end. He was now enveloped, enfolded. Already everything to him—even his love for Margaret—was trivial in comparison with the effect of some atmosphere that was beginning to hem him in on every side.

But against all this was the other Olva—the Olva who desired physical strength, love, freedom, health.

Well, let it all be as confusing as it might, he would play his game. But as he walked into the Pavilion he knew that the prelude to his real life had only a few more hours to run. . . .

IV

As he passed, with the rest of the team, up the field, he observed two things only; one thing was Margaret, standing on the left side of the field just below the covered stand—he could see her white face and her little black hard hat.

The other thing was that on the horizon where the wall at the further end of the field cut the sky there were piled, as though resting on the top of the wall, high white clouds. For a moment these clouds, piled in mountain shape of an intense whiteness with round curving edges, held his eyes because they exactly resembled those clouds that had hung above him on the day of his walk to Sannet Wood—the day when he had been caught by the snowstorm. These clouds brooded, waiting above him; their dazzling white had the effect of a steady, unswerving gaze.

They lined out. He took his place as centre three-quarter with Cardillac outside left and Tester and Buchan on the other wing. Old Lawrence was standing, a solid rock of a figure, back. There was a great crowd present. The tops of the hansom cabs in the road beyond rose above the wall, and he could hear, muffled with distance, shots from the 'Varsity firing range.

All these things focussed themselves upon his brain in the moment before the whistle went; the whistle blew, the Dublin men had kicked off, Tester had fielded the ball, sent it back into touch, and the game had begun.

This was to be the game of his life and yet he could not centre his attention upon it. He was conscious that Whymper—the great Whymper—was acting as linesman and watching every movement. He knew that for most of that great crowd his was the figure that was of real concern, he knew that he was as surely battling for his lady as though he had been fighting, tournament-wise, six hundred years ago.

But it all seemed of supreme unimportance. To-night he was to face Rupert, to state, once and for all, that he had killed Carfax, to submit Margaret to a terrible test . . . even that of no importance. All life was insignificant beside something that was about to happen; before the gaze of that white dazzling cloud be felt that he stood, a little pigmy, alone on a brown spreading field.

The game was up at the University end. The Dublin men were pressing and the Cambridge forwards seemed to have lost their heads. It was a case now of "scrum," lining out, and "scrum" again. The Cambridge men got the ball, kept it between their heels and tried, desperately to wheel with it and carry it along with them. It escaped them, dribbled out of the scrimmage, the Cambridge half leapt upon it, but the Dublin man was upon him before he could get it away. It was on the ground again, the Dublin forwards dribbled it a little and then some one, sweeping it into his arms, fell forward with it, over the line, the Cambridge men on top of him.

Dublin had scored a try, and a goal from an easy angle followed—Dublin five points.

They all moved back to the centre of the field and now the Cambridge men, rushing the ball from a line-out in their favour, pressed hard. At last the ball came to the three-quarters. Tester caught it, it passed to Buchan, who as he fell flung it right out to Cardillac; Cardillac draw his man, swerved, and sent it back to Olva. As Olva felt the neat hard surface of it, as he knew that the way was almost clear before him, his feet seemed clogged with heavy weights. Something was about to happen to him—something, but not this. The crowd behind the ropes were shouting, he knew that he was himself running, but it seemed that only his body was moving, his real self was standing back, gazing at those white clouds—waiting.

He knew that he made no attempt to escape the man in front of him; he seemed to run straight into his arms; he heard a little sigh go up from behind the ropes, as he tumbled to the ground, letting the ball trickle feebly from his fingers. A try missed if ever one was!

No one said anything, but he felt the disappointment in the air. He knew what they were saying—"One of Dune's off days! I always said you couldn't depend upon the man. He's just too sidey to care what happens. . . ."

Well they might say it if they would; his eyes were on the horizon.

But his failure had had its effect. Let there be an individualist in the line and Tester and Buchan would play their well-ordered game to perfection. They relied as a rule upon Whymper—to-day they had depended upon Dune. Well Dune had failed them, the forwards were heeling so slowly, the scrum-half was never getting the ball away—it was a miserable affair.

The Dublin forwards pressed again. For a long time the two bodies of men swayed backwards and forwards; in the University twenty-five Lawrence was performing wonders. He seemed to be everywhere at once, bringing men down, seizing, in a lightning flash of time, his opportunity for relieving by kicking into touch.

Twice the ball went to the Dublin three-quarters and they seemed certainly in, but on the first occasion a man slipped and on the second Olva caught his three-quarter and brought him sharply to the ground. It was the only piece of work that he had done.

More struggling—then away on the right some Dublin man had caught it and was running. Some one dashed at him to hurl him into touch, but he slipped past and was in.

Another try—the kick was again successful—Dublin ten points.

The half-time whistle blew. As the met gathered into groups in the middle of the field, sucking lemons and gathering additional melancholy there from, Olva stood a little away from them. Whymper came out into the field to exhort and advise. As he passed Olva he said—

"Rather missed that try of yours. Ought to have gone a bit faster."

He did not answer, it seemed to be no concern of his at all. He was now trembling it every limb, but his excitement had nothing to do with the game. It seemed to him that the earth and the sky were sharing his emotion am he could feel in the air a great exaltation. I was becoming literally true for him that earth air, sky were praising at this moment, in wonderful unison, some great presence.

"All things betray Thee who betrayest Me. . . ." Now he understood what that line had intended him to feel—the very sods crushed by his boots were leading him to submission.

The whistle sounded. His back now was turned to the white clouds; he was facing the high stone wall and the tops of the hansom cabs.

The game began again. The Dublin men were determined to drive their advantage to victory. Another goal and their lead might settle, once and for all, the issue.

Olva was standing back, listening. The earth was humming like a top. A voice seemed to be borne on the wind—"Coming, Coming, Coming."

He felt that the clouds were spreading behind him and a little wind seemed to be whispering in the grass—"Coming, Coming, Coming." His very existence now was strung to a pitch of expectation.

As in a dream he saw that a Dublin man with the ball had got clear away from the clump of Cambridge forwards, and was coming towards him. Behind him only was Lawrence. He flung himself at the man's knees, caught them, falling himself desperately forward. They both came crashing to the ground. It was a magnificent collar, and Olva, as he fell, heard, as though it were miles away, a rising shout, saw the sky bend down to him, saw the ball as it was jerked up rise for a moment into the air—was conscious that some one was running.

V

He was on his knees, alone, on the vast field that sloped a little towards the horizon.

Before him the mountain clouds were now lit with a clear silver light so dazzling that his eyes were lowered.

About him was a great silence. He was himself minute in size, a tiny, tiny bending figure.

Many years passed.

A great glory caught the colour from the sky and earth and held it like a veil before the cloud.

In a voice of the most radiant happiness Olva cried—

"I have fled—I am caught—I am held . . . Lord, I submit."

And for the second time he heard God's voice—

"My Son . . . My Son."

He felt a touch—very gentle and tender—on his shoulder.

VI

Many years had passed. He opened his eyes and saw the ball that had been rising, many years ago, now falling.

The man whom he had collared was climbing to his feet; behind them men were bending down for a "scrum." The shout that he had heard when he had fallen was still lingering in the air.

And yet many years had passed.

"Hope you're not hurt," the Dublin man said. "Came down hard."

"No, thanks, it's all right."

Olva got on to his feet. Some one cried, "Well collared, Dune."

He ran back to his place. Now there was no hesitation or confusion. A vigour like wine filled his body. The Cambridge men now were pressing; the ball was flung back to Cardillac, who threw to Olva. The Dublin line was only a few yards away and Olva was over. Lawrence kicked a goal and Cambridge had now five points to the Dublin ten.

Cambridge now awoke to its responsibilities. The Dublin men seemed to be flagging a little, and Tester and Buchan, having apparently decided that Olva was himself again, played their accustomed game.

But what had happened to Dune? There he had been his old casual superior self during the first half of the game. Now he was that inspired player that the Harlequin match had once revealed him. Whymper had spoken to him at half-time. That was what it was—Whymper had roused him.

For he was amazing. He was everywhere. Even when he had been collared, he was suddenly up, had raced after the three-quarter line, caught them up and was in the movement again. Five times the Cambridge Threes were going, were half-way down the field, and were checked by the wonderful Dublin defence. Again and again Cambridge pressed. There were only ten minutes left for play and Cambridge were still five points behind.

Somebody standing in the crowd said, "By Jove, Dune seems to be enjoying it. I never saw any one look as happy."

Some one else said, "Dune's possessed by a devil or something. I never saw anything like that pace. He doesn't seem to be watching the game at all, though."

Some one said, "There's going to be a tremendous snowstorm in a minute. Look at those white clouds."

Then, when there were five minutes more to play, there was a forward rush over the Dublin line—a Cambridge man, struggling at the bottom of a heap of legs and arms, touched down. A Dublin appeal was made for "Carried over," but—no—"Try for Cambridge."

A deafening shout from behind the ropes, then a breathless pause whilst Lawrence stepped back to take the kick, then a shattering roar as the ball sailed between the posts.

Ten points all and three minutes left to play.

They were back to the centre, the Dublin men had kicked, Tester had gathered and returned to touch. There was a line-out, a Cambridge man had the ball and fell, Cambridge dribbled past the ball to the half, the ball was in Cardillac's hands.

Let this be ever to Cardillac's honour! Fame of a lifetime might have been his, the way was almost clear before him—he passed back to Olva. The moment had come. The crowd fell first into a breathless silence, then screamed with excitement—

"Dune's got it. He's off!"

He had a crowd of men upon him. Handing off, bending, doubling, almost down, slipping and then up again—he was through them.

The great clouds were gathering the grey sky into their white arms. Mr. Gregg, at the back of the stand, forgetting for once decorum, white and trembling, was hoarse with shouting.

Olva's body seemed so tiny on that vast field—two Dublin three-quarters came for him. He appeared to run straight into the arms of both of them and then was through them. They started after him—one man was running across field to catch him. It was a race. Now there fell silence as the three men tore after the flying figure. Surely never, in the annals of Rugby football, had any one run as Olva ran then. Only now the Dublin back, and he, missing the apparent swerve to the right, clutched desperately at Olva's back, caught the buckle of his "shorts" and stood with the thing torn off in his hand.

He turned to pursue, but it was too late. Olva had touched down behind the posts.

As he started back with the ball the wide world seemed to be crying and shouting, waving and screaming.

Against the dull grey sky far away an ancient cabman, standing on the top of his hansom, flourished his whip.

But as he stood there the shouting died—the crowds faded—alone there on the brown field with the white high clouds above him, Olva was conscious, only, of the gentle touch of a hand on his shoulder.

CHAPTER XV

I

He had a bath, changed his clothes, and sitting before his fire waited.

As he looked around his room he knew that he was leaving it for ever. What ever might be the issue of his conversation with Rupert, he knew that that at any rate was true; he would never return here again—or he would not return until he had worked out his duty. He looked about him regretfully; he had grown very fond of that room and the things in it—the shape of it, the books, the blue bowls, the bright fire, "Aegidius" (but he would take "Aegidius" with him). He looked last at the photograph of his father, the rocky eyes, the flowing beard, the massive shoulders.

It was back to him that he was going, and he would walk all the way. Walking alone he would listen, he would watch, he would wait, and then, in that great silence, he would be told what he must do.

In the pleasant crackle of the fire, in the shaded light of the lamp, in the starlit silence of the College Courts, there seemed such safety; in his heart there was such happiness; in that moment of waiting for Rupert Craven to come he learnt once and for all that, in very truth, there is no gift, no reward, no joy that can equal "the Peace of God," nor is there any temporal danger, disease or agony that can threaten its power.

As the last notes of the clock in Outer Court striking five died away Rupert Craven came in. If he had seemed tired and worn-out before, now the overwhelming impression that he gave was of an unhappiness from which he seemed to have no outlet. He was young enough to be tormented by the determination to do the right thing; he was young enough to give his whole devotion to his sister; he was young enough to admire, against all determination, Olva's presence and prowess and silence; he was young enough to be haunted, night and day, by the terrors of his imagination; he was young enough to be amazed at finding the world a place of Life and Death; he was young enough finally to be staggered that he personally should be drawn into the struggle.

But now, just now, as he stood in the doorway, he was simply tired, tired out. He pulled himself together with the obvious intention of being cold and fierce and judicial. He had cornered Dune at last, he had driven him to confession, he was a fine fellow, a kind of Fate, the Supreme Judge . . . this is what he doubtless desired to feel; but he wished that Dune had not played so wonderful a game that afternoon, that Dune did not now—at this moment of complete disaster and ruin—look so strangely happy, that he were himself not so utterly wretched and conscious of his own failure to do anything as it ought to be done. He did his best; he refused to sit down, he remained as still as possible, he looked over Dune's head in order to avoid those shining eyes.

The eyes caught him.

"Craven, why have you been badgering the wretched Bunning?"

"I thought you asked me to come here to tell me something—I didn't come to answer questions."

"We'll come to my part of it in a moment. But I think it's only fair to answer me first."

"What have you got to do with Bunning?"

"That's not, immediately, the point. The thing I want to know is, why you should have chosen, during the last week, to go and torment the hapless Bunning until you've all but driven him out of his wits."

"I don't see what it's got to do with you."

"It's got this much to do with me—that he came to me this morning with a story so absurd that it proves that he can't be altogether right in his head. He told me that he had confided this absurd story to you."

There was no answer.

"I don't suppose," Olva went on at last gently, "that we've either of us got very much time, and there's a great deal to be done, so let's go straight to it. Bunning told me this morning that he declared to you yesterday that he—of all people in the world—had murdered Carfax."

"Yes," at last Craven sullenly muttered, "he told me that."

"And of course you didn't believe it?"

"I didn't believe that he'd done it—no. But he knows who did do it. He's got all the details. Some one has told him."

Craven was trembling. Olva pushed a chair towards him.

"Look here, you'd better sit down."

Craven sat down.

"I know that some one told him," Olva said quietly, "because I told him."

"Then you know who—" Craven's voice was a whisper.

"I know," said Olva, "because it was I who killed Carfax."

Craven took it—the moment for which he'd been waiting so long—in the most amazing way.

"Oh!" he cried, like a child who has cut its finger. "Oh! I wish you hadn't!" There was the whole of Craven's young struggle with an astounding world in that cry.

Then, after that, there was a long silence, and had some one come into the room he would have looked at the two men before the fire and have supposed that they were gently and comfortably falling off to sleep.

Olva at last said; "Of course I know that you have suspected me for a long time. Everything played into your hands. I have done my very utmost to prevent your having positive proof of the thing, but that part of the business is now done with. You know, and you can do what you please with the knowledge."

But, now that the moment had come, Rupert Craven could do nothing with it.

"I don't want to do anything," he muttered at last. "I'm not up to doing anything. I don't understand it. I'm not the sort of fellow who ought to be in this kind of thing at all."

That was how he now saw it, as an unfair advantage that had been taken of him. This point of view changed his position to the extent of his now almost appealing to Olva to help him out of it.

"Your telling me like that has made it all so difficult. I feel now suddenly as though I hated Carfax and hadn't the least objection to somebody doing for him. And that's all wrong—murder's an awful thing— one ought to feel bad about it." Then finally, with the cry of a child in the dark, "But this isn't life, it never has been life since that day I heard of Carfax being killed. It's the sort of thing—it's been for weeks the sort of thing—that you read of in books or see at the Adelphi; and I'm not that kind of fellow. I tell you I've been mad all this last month, getting it on the brain, seeing things night and day. My one idea was to make you own up to it, but I never thought of what was going to happen when you did."

Olva let him work it out.

"Of course I never thought of you for an instant as the man until that afternoon when you talked in your sleep. Then I began to think and I remembered what Carfax had said about your hating him. Then I went with your dog for a walk and we found your matchbox. After that I noticed all sorts of things and, at the same time, I saw that you were in love with Margaret. That made me mad. My sister is everything in the world to me, and it seemed to me that—she should marry a fellow who . . . without knowing! I began to be ill with it and yet I hadn't any real reasons to bring forward. You wanted me to show my cards, but I wouldn't. Sometimes I thought I really was going mad. Then two things made me desperate. I saw that you had some secret understanding with my mother and I saw—that my sister loved you. We'd always been tremendous pals—we three, and it seemed as though every one were siding against me. I saw Margaret marrying you and mother letting her—although she knew . . . it was awful—Hell!"

He pressed his hands together, his voice shook: "I'd never been in anything before—no kind of trouble— and now it seemed to put me right on one side. I couldn't see straight. One moment I hated you, then I admired you, and the oddest thing of all was that I didn't think about the actual thing—your having killed Carfax—at all; everything else was so much more important. I just wanted to be sure that you'd done it and then—for you to go away and never see any of us again."

Olva smiled.

"Yes," he said.

"But it wasn't until the 5th of November—the 'rag' night—that I was quite sure. I knew then, when I saw you hitting that fellow, that you'd killed Carfax. But, of course, that wasn't proof. Then I noticed Bunning. I saw that he was always with you, and of course it was an odd sort of friendship for you to have; I could see, too, that he'd got something on his mind. I went for him—it was all easy enough—and at last he broke down. Then I'd got you—"

"You've got me," said Olva.

Rupert looked him, slowly, in the face. "You're wonderful!" Then he added, almost wistfully, "If Margaret hadn't loved you it wouldn't really any of it have mattered. I suppose that's very immoral, but that's what it comes to. Margaret's everything in the world to me and you must tell her."

"Of course I will tell her," Olva said. "That's what I ought to have done from the beginning. That's what I was meant to do. But I had to be driven to it. What will you do, Craven, if it doesn't matter to her—if she doesn't care whether I killed Carfax or no?"

"At least you'll have told her," the boy replied firmly. "At least she'll know. Then it's for her to decide. She'll do the right thing," he ended proudly.

"And what do you think that is?" Olva asked him.

"I don't know," he answered. "This seems to have altered everything. I ought now to be hating you—I don't. I ought to shudder at the sight of you—I don't. The Carfax business seems to have slipped right back, to be ages ago, not to matter. All I suppose I wanted was to be reassured about you—if Margaret loved you. And now I am reassured. I believe you know what to do."

"Yes, I know what to do," said Olva. "I'm going away to-morrow for a long time. I shall always love Margaret—there can never be any one else—but I shall not marry her unless I can come back cleared."

"And who—what—can clear you?"

"Ah! who knows! There'll be something for me to do, I expect. . . . I will see Margaret to-morrow—and say good-bye."

Craven's face was white, the eyelids had almost closed, his head hung forward as though it were too heavy to support.

"I'm just about done," he murmured, "just about done. It's been all a beastly dream . . . and now you're all right—you and Margaret—I haven't got to bother about her any more."

II

After hall Olva went to Cardillac's room for the last time. No one there knew that it was for the last time. It seemed to them all that he was just beginning to come out, to be one of them. The football match of that afternoon had been wonderful enough for anything, and the excitement of it lingered still about Cardillac's rooms, thick now with tobacco-smoke, crowded with men, noisy with laughter. The air was so strong with smoke, the lights so dim, the voices so many, that Olva finding a corner near an open window slipped, it might almost seem, from the world. Outside the snow, threatening all day, now fell heavily; the old Court took it with a gentleness that showed that the snow was meant for it, and the snow covered the grey roofs and the smooth grass with a satisfaction that could almost be heard, so deep was it. Just this little window-pane between the world that Olva was leaving and the world to which he was going!

He caught fragments: "Just that last run—gorgeous—but old Snodky says that that horse of his—"

"My dear fellow, you take it from me—they can't get on without it. . . . Now a girl I know—"

"They fairly fell upon one another's necks and hugged. Talk of the fatted calf! Now if I'd asked the governor—"

Around him there came, with a poignancy, a beauty, that, now that he was to lose it all, was like a wound, the wonder of this Cambridge. Then he had it, the marvellous moment! On the other side of the window the still court, a few twinkling lights, the powdering snow—and here the vitality, the energy, the glowing sense of two thousand souls marching together upon Life and seizing it, with a shout, lifting it, stepping out with it as though it were one long glory! Afterwards what matter? There had been the moment, never to be forgotten! Cambridge, the beautiful threshold!

For an instant the sense of his own forthcoming journey—away from life, as it seemed to him—caught him as he sat there. "What will God do with me?"

From the outer world through the whispering snow, he caught the echo of the Voice—"My Son . . . My Son."

Soon he heard Lawrence's tremendous laugh—"Where's Dune? Is he here?"

Lawrence found him and sat down beside him.

"By Jupiter, old man, I was frightened for you this afternoon. Until half-time you were drugged or somethin', and there was I prayin' to my Druids all I was worth to put back into you. And, my word, they did it I Talk about that second half—never saw anythin' like it! Have a drink, old man!"

"No, thanks. Yes, I didn't seem to get on to it at all at first."

"Well, you're fixed for Queen's Club—just heard—got your Blue all right. You and Whymper ought to do fine things between you, although stickin' two individualists together on the same wing like that ain't exactly my idea, and they don't as a rule settle the team as early as this"—Lawrence put a large hand on Olva's knee. "Goin' home for Christmas?" he said.

"I expect so."

"Well, yer see—I've got a sort of idea. I wish this vac, you'd come an' stay with us for a bit. Good old sorts, my people. Governor quite a brainy man—and you could talk, you two. There'll be lots of people tumblin' about the place—lots goin' on, and the governor'll like to have a sensible feller once in a way . . . and I'd like it too," he ended at the bottom of his gruff voice.

"Well, you see;" Olva explained, "it depends a bit on my own father. He's all alone up there at our place, and I like to be with him as much as possible." Olva looked through the window at the snow, grey against the sky, white against the college walls. "I don't quite know where I shall be—I think you must let me write to you."

"Oh! that's all right," said Lawrence. "I want you to come along some time. You'd like the governor—and if you don't mind listening to an ass like me—well, I'd take it as an honour if you'd talk to me a bit."

As Olva looked Lawrence in the eyes he knew that it would be well with him if, in his journey through the world, he met again so good a soul. Cardillac joined them and they all talked for a little. Then Olva said good-night.

He turned for a moment at the door and looked back. Some one at the other end of the room was singing "Egypt" to a cracked piano. A babel of laughter, of chatter, every now and again men tumbled against one another, like cubs in a cave, and rolled upon the floor. Lawrence, his feet planted wide apart, was standing in the middle of an admiring circle, explaining something very slowly.

"If the old scrum-half," he was saying, "only stood back enough—"

What a splendid lot they were! What a life it was! So much joy in the heart of so much beauty! . . . Cambridge!

As he crossed the white court the strains of "Egypt" came, like a farewell, through the tumbling snow.

There was still a thing that he must do. He went to say good-bye to Bunning. He thought with surprise as he climbed the stairs that this was the first time that he'd ever been to Bunning's room. It had always been Bunning who had come to him. He would always see that picture—Bunning standing, clumsily, awkwardly in the doorway. Poor Bunning!

When Olva came in he was sitting in a very old armchair, staring into the fire, his hair on end and his tie above his collar. Olva watched him for a moment, the face, the body, everything about him utterly dejected; the sound of Olva's entrance did not at once rouse him. When at last he saw who it was he started up, his face flushing crimson.

"You!" he cried.

"Yes," said Olva, "I've come to tell you that everything's all right."

For a moment light touched Bunning's eyes, then slowly he shook his head.

"Things can't be all right. It's gone much too far."

"My dear Bunning, I've seen Craven. I've told him. I assure you that all is well."

"You told him?"

"Everything. That I killed Carfax—he knew it, of course, long ago. He went fast asleep at the end of it."

Bunning shook his head again, wearily. "It's all no good. You're saying these things to comfort me. Even if Craven didn't do anything he wouldn't let you marry his sister now. That's more important than being hung."

"If it hadn't been for you," Olva said slowly, "I should have gone on wriggling. You've made me come out into the open. 'I'm going to tell Miss Craven everything to-morrow."

"What will she do?"

"I don't know. She'll do the right thing. After that I'm going away."

"Going away?"

"Yes. I want to think about things. I've never thought about anything except myself. I'm going to tramp it home, and after that I shall find out what I'm going to do."

"And Miss Craven?"

"I shall come back to her one day—when I'm fit for it—or rather, if I'm fit for it. But that's enough about myself. I only wanted to tell you, Bunning, before I go that I shall never forget your telling Craven. You're lucky to have been able to do so fine a thing. We shall meet again later on—I'll see to that."

Bunning, his whole body strung to a desperate appeal, caught Olva's hand. "Take me with you, Dune. Take me with you. I'll be your servant—anything you like. I'll do anything if you'll let me come. I won't be a nuisance—I'll never talk if you don't want me to—I'll do everything you tell me—only let me come. You're the only person who's ever shown me what I might do. I might be of use if I were with you—otherwise—"

"Rot, Bunning. You've got plenty to do here. I'm no good yet for anybody. One day perhaps we'll meet again. I'll write to you. I promise not to forget you. How could I? and one day I'll come back—"

Bunning moved away, his head banging. "You must think me an awful fool—of course you do. I am, I suppose. I'd be awful to be with for long at a time—of course I see that. But I don't know what to do. If I go home and tell them I'm not going to be a parson it'll be terrible. They'll all be at me. Not directly. They won't say anything, but they'll have people to talk to me. They'll fill the house—they won't spare any pains. And then, at last, being all alone, I shall give in. I know I shall, I'm not clever or strong. And I shall be ordained—and then it'll be hell. I can see it all. You came into my life and made it all different, and now you're going out of it again and it will be worse than ever—"

"I won't go out of it," said Olva. "I'll write if you'd like—and perhaps we'll meet. I'll be always your friend. And—look here—I'll tell Margaret—Miss Craven—about you, and she'll ask you to go and see her, and if you two are friends it'll be a kind of alliance between all of us, won't it?"

Bunning was happier—"Oh, but she'll think me such an ass!"

"Oh no, she won't, she's much too clever, And, Bunning, don't let yourself be driven by people. Stick to the thing you want to do—you'll find something all right. Just go on here and wait until you're shown. Sit with your ears open—"

Bunning filled his mouth with toast. "If you'll write to me and keep up with me I'll do anything."

"And one thing—Don't tell any one I'm going. I shall just slip out of college early the day after to-morrow. I don't want any one to know. It's nobody's affair but mine."

Then he held out his hand—"Good-bye, Bunning, old man."

"Good-bye," said Bunning.

When Olva had gone he sat down by the fire again, staring.

Some hours afterwards he spoke, suddenly, aloud: "I can stand the lot of them now."

Then he went to bed.

CHAPTER XVI

OLVA AND MARGARET

I

On the next evening the sun set with great splendour. The frost had come and hardened the snow and all day the sky bad been a pale frozen blue, only on the horizon fading into crocus yellow.

The sun was just vanishing behind the grey roofs when Olva went to Rocket Road. All day he had been very busy destroying old letters and papers and seeing to everything so that he should leave no untidiness nor carelessness behind him. Now it was all over. To-morrow morning, with enough money but not very much, and with an old rucksack that he had once had on a walking tour, he would set out. He did not question this decision—he knew that it was what he was intended to do—but it was the way that Margaret would take his confession that would make that journey hard or easy.

He did not know—that was the surprising thing—how she would take it. He knew her so little. He only knew that he loved her and that she would do, without flinching, the thing that she felt was right. Oh! but it would be difficult!

The house, the laurelled drive, the little road, the distant moor and wood—these things had to-night a gentle air. Over the moor the setting sun flung a red flame; the woods burned black; the laurels were heavy with snow and a robin hopped down the drive as Olva passed.

He found Margaret in the drawing-room, and here, too, he fancied that there was more light and air than on other days.

When the old woman had left the room he suddenly caught Margaret to him and kissed her as though he would never let her go. She clung to him with her hands. Then he stood gravely away from her.

"There," he said, "that is the last time that I may kiss you before I have told you what it is that I have come here to say. But first may I go up to your mother for a moment?"

"Yes," Margaret said, "if you will not be very long. I do not think that I can have much more patience." Then she added more slowly, gazing into his face, "Rupert said last night that you would have something to tell me to-day. I have been waiting all day for you to come. But Rupert was his old self last night, and he talked to mother and has made her happy again. Oh! I think that everything is going to be right!"

"I will soon come down to you," he said.

Mrs. Craven's long dark room was lit by the setting sun; beyond her windows the straight white fields lifted shining splendour to the stars already twinkling in the pale sky. Candles were lit on a little black table by her sofa and the fire was red deep in its cavernous setting.

He stood for a moment in the dim room facing the setting sun, and the light of the fire played about his feet and the pale glow that stole up into the evening from the snowy fields touched his face.

She knew as she looked at him that something bad given him great peace.

"I've come to say good-bye," he said. Then he sat down by her side.

"No," she said, smiling, "you mustn't go. We want you—Rupert and Margaret and I. . . ." Then softly, as though to herself, she repeated the words, "Rupert and Margaret and I."

"Dear Mrs. Craven, one day I will come back. But tell me, Rupert spoke to you last night?"

"Yes, he has made me so very happy. Last night we were the same again as we used to be, and even, I think, more than we have ever been. Rupert is growing up."

"Yes—Rupert is growing up. Did he tell you why he had, during these weeks, been so strange and unhappy?"

"No, he gave me no real explanation. But I think that it was the terrible death of his friend Mr. Carfax—I think that that had preyed upon his mind."

"No, Mrs. Craven, it was more than that. He was unhappy because he knew that it was I that had killed Carfax."

He saw a little movement pass over her—her hand trembled against her dress. For some time they sat together there in silence, and the red sun slipped down behind the fields; the room was suddenly dark except for the yellow pool of light that the candles made and for the strange gleam by the window that came from the snow.

At last she said, "Now I understand—now I understand."

"I killed him in anger—it was quite fair. No one had any idea except Rupert, but everything helped to show him that it was I. When he saw that I loved Margaret he was very unhappy. He saw that we had some kind of understanding together and he thought that I had told you and that you sympathize with me. I am going down now to tell Margaret."

"Poor, poor Olva." It was the first time that she had called him by his Christian name. She took his hand. "Both of us together—the same thing. I have paid, God knows I have paid, and soon, I hope, it will be over. But your life is before you."

He looked out at the evening fields. "I'm going down now to tell Margaret. And tomorrow I shall set out. I will not come back to Margaret until I know that I am cleared—but I want you, while I am away, to think of me sometimes and to talk of me sometimes to Margaret. And one day, perhaps, I shall know that I may come back."

She put her thin hands about his head and drew it down to her and kissed him.

"There will never be a time when you are not in my mind," she said. "I love you as though you were my own son. I had hoped that you would be here often, but now I see that it is right for you to go. I know that Margaret will wait for you. Meanwhile an old woman loves you."

He kissed her and left her.

At the door through the dark room he heard her thin voice: "May God bless you and keep you."

He went to perform his hardest task.

II

It was the harder in that for a little while he seemed to be left absolutely alone. The room was dark save for the leaping light of the fire in the deep stone fireplace, and as he saw Margaret standing there waiting for him, desperately courageous, he only knew that he loved her so badly that, for a little while, he could only stand there staring at her, twisting his hands together, speechless.

"Well," at last she said. "Come and sit down and tell me all about it." But her voice trembled a little and her eyes were wide, frightened, begging him not to hurt her.

He sat down near her, before the fire, and she instinctively, as though she knew that this was a very tremendous matter, stood away from him, her hands clasped together against her black dress.

Suddenly now, before he spoke, he realized what it would mean to him if she could not forgive what he had done. He had imagined it once before—the slow withdrawal of her eyes, the gradual tightening of the lips, the little instinctive movement away from him.

If he must go out into the world, having lost her, he thought that he could never endure, God or no God, the long dreary years in front of him.

At last he was brave: "Margaret—at first I want you to know that I love you with all my heart and soul and body; that nothing that can ever happen to me can ever alter that love—that I am yours, entirely, always. And then I want you to know that I am not worthy to love you, that I ought never to have asked you to love me, that I ought to have gone away the first time that I saw you."

She made a little loving, protecting movement towards him with her hands and then let them drop against her dress again.

"I ought never to have loved you—because—only a day or two before I met you—I had killed Carfax, Rupert's friend."

The words as they fell seemed to him like the screams that iron bolts give as a gate is barred.

He whispered slowly the words again: "I killed Carfax"—and then he covered his eyes with his hands so that he might not see her face.

The silence seemed eternal—and she had made no movement. To fill that silence he went on desperately—

"I had always hated him—there were many reasons—and one day we met in Sannet Wood, quarrelled, and I hit him. The blow killed him. I don't think I meant to kill him, but I wasn't sorry afterwards—I have never felt remorse for that. There have been other things. . . .

"Soon afterwards I met you—I loved you at once—you know that I did—and I could not tell you. Oh! I tried—I struggled, pretty poor struggling—but I could not. I thought that it was all over, that he was dead and nobody knew. But God was wiser than that—Rupert knew. He suspected and then he grew more sure, and at last he was quite certain. Yesterday, after the football match, I told him and I promised him that I would tell you . . . and I have told you."

Silence again—and then suddenly there was movement, and there were arms about him and a voice in his ear—"Poor, poor Olva . . . dear Olva . . . how terrible it must have been!"

He could only then catch her and hold her, and furiously press her against him. "Oh, my dear, my dear—you don't mind!"

They stayed together, like that, for a long time.

He could not think clearly, but in the dim recesses of his mind he saw that they had all—Mrs. Craven, Margaret, Rupert—taken it in the same kind of way. Could it be that Margaret and Rupert living, although unconsciously, in the shadow all their lives of just this crime, breathing the air of it, and breathing it too with the other air of love and affection—that they had thus, all unknowing, been quietly prepared?

Or had they, each of them, their especial reason for excusing it? Mrs. Craven from her great knowledge, Rupert from his great weariness, Margaret from her great love?

At last Margaret got up and sat down in a chair away from him.

"Olva dear, you ought to have told me. If we had married and you had not told me—"

"I was so terribly afraid of losing you."

"But it gives me now," her voice was almost triumphant, "something to share with you, something to help you in, something to fight with you. Now I can show you how much I love you.

"How could you have supposed that I would mind? Do you think that a woman, if she loves a man, cares for anything that he may do? If you had killed a hundred men in Sannet Wood I would have helped you to bury them. The thing that a woman demands most of love is that she may prove it. I know that murder has a dreadful sound—but to meet your enemy face to face, to strike him down because you hated him—" Her voice rose, her eyes flashed—she raised her arms—"You must pay for it, Olva—but we shall pay together."

He knew now, as he watched her, that he had a harder thing to do than he had believed possible.

"No," he said, and his eyes could not face hers, "we can't pay together—I must go alone."

She laughed a little. "How can you go alone if we are together?"

"We shall not be together. I go away, alone, to-morrow."

He knew that her eyes were then, very slowly, searching his face. She said, gently, after a moment's pause, "Tell me, Olva, what you mean. Of course we are going together."

"Oh, it is so hard for me!" He was fighting now as he had never fought. Why not, even at this last moment, in spite of yesterday, defy God and stay with her and keep her? In that moment of hesitation he suffered so that the sweat came to his forehead and his eyes were filled with pain and then were suddenly tired and dull.

But he came out, and seemed now to stand above the room and look down on his body and her body and to be filled with a great pity for them both.

"Margaret dear, it's very hard for me to tell you. Will you be patient with me and let me put things as clearly as I can—as I see them?"

She burst out, "Olva, you mustn't leave me, I—" Then she used all her strength to bring control. Very quietly she ended—"Yes, Olva, tell me everything."

"It is so difficult because it is about God, and we all of us feel, and rightly I expect, that it is priggish to talk about God at all. And then I don't know whether I can give you everything as it happened because it was all so unsubstantial and at the end of it any one might say 'But this is nothing—nothing at all. You've been hysterical, nervous—that's the meaning of it. You've nothing to show.' And yet if all the world were to say that to me I should still have no doubt. I know, as I know that we are sitting here, as I know that I love you, that what I say is true."

She brought her chair close to him and then put her band in his and waited.

"After I had killed Carfax—after his body had fallen and the wood was very silent, I was suddenly conscious of God. I can't explain that better. I can only say that I knew that some one had watched me, I knew that the world would never be the same place again because some one had watched me, and I knew that it was not because I had done wrong, but because I had put myself into a new set of conditions that life would be different now. I knew these things, and I went back to College.

"I had never thought about God before, never at all. I had been entirely heathen. Now I was sure of His existence in the way that one is sure of wood when one touches it or water when one drinks it.

"But I did not know at all what kind of God He was. I went to a Revival meeting, but He was not there. He was not in the College Chapel. He was not in any forms or ceremonies that I could discover. He might choose to appear to other men in those different ways but not to me. Then a fellow, Lawrence, told me about some old worship—Druids and their altars—but He was not there. And all those days I was increasingly conscious that there was some one who would not let me alone. It fastened itself in my mind gradually as a Pursuit, and it seemed to me too that, as the days passed, I began slowly to understand the nature of the Pursuer—that He was kind and tender but also relentless, remorseless. I was frightened. I flung myself into College things—games and every kind of noise because I was so afraid of silence. And all the time some one urged me to obedience. That was all that He demanded, that I should be passive and obey His orders. I would have given in, I think, very soon, but I met you."

Her hand tightened in his and then, because he felt that her body was trembling, he put his arm round her and held her.

"I knew then when I loved you that I was being urged, by this God, to confess everything to you. I became frightened; I should have trusted you, but it was so great a risk. You were all that I had and if I lost you life would have gone too. Those aren't mere words. . . . I struggled, I tried every way of escape. And then everything betrayed me. Rupert began to suspect, then to be sure. Whether I flung myself into everything or hid in my room it was the same—God came closer and closer. It was a perfectly real experience and I could see Him as a great Shadow—not unkind, loving me, but relentless. Then the day came that I proposed to you and I fainted. I knew then that I was not to be allowed so easy a happiness. Still I struggled, but now God seemed to have shut off all the real world and only left me the unreal one—and I began to be afraid that I was going mad."

She suddenly bent down and kissed him; she stayed then, until he had finished, with her head buried in his coat.

"It wasn't any good—I knew all the time that it could only end one way.

"Everything betrayed me, every one left me. I thought every moment that Rupert would tell me. Then, one night when I was hardly sane, I told a man, Bunning—a queer odd creature who was the last kind of person to be told. He, in a fit of mad self-sacrifice, told Rupert that he'd killed Carfax, and then of course it was all over.

"I suddenly yielded. It was as though God caught me and held me. I saw Him, I heard Rim—yesterday—in the middle of the football. I know that it was so. After that there could be only one thing—Obedience. I knew that I must tell you. I have told you. I know, too, that I must go out into the world, alone, and work out my duty . . . and then, oh! then, I will come back."

When he had finished, on his shoulder he seemed to feel once more a hand gently resting.

At last she raised her head, and clutching his hand as though she would never let it go, spoke:—

"Olva, Olva, I don't understand. I don't think I believe in any God. And, dear, see—it is all so natural. Thinking about what you had done, thinking of it all alone, preyed on your nerves. Because Rupert suspected you made it worse. You imagined things—everything. That is all—Olva, really that is all."

"Margaret, don't make it harder for both of us. I must go. There is no question. I don't suppose that any one can see any one else's spiritual experiences—one must be alone in that. Margaret dear, if I stayed with you now—if we married—the Pursuit would begin again. God would hold me at last—and then one day you would find that I had gone away—I would have been driven—there would be terror for both of us then."

She slipped on to her knees and caught his hands.

"This is all unreal—utterly unreal. But our love for each other, that is the only thing that can matter for either of us. You have lived in your thoughts these weeks, imagined things, but think of what you do if you leave me. You are all I have—you have become my world—I can't live, I can't live, Olva, without you."

"I must go. I must find what God is."

"But listen, dear. You come to me to confess something. You find that what you have done matters nothing to me. You say that you love me more than ever, and, in the same moment, that you are going to leave me. Is it fair to me? You give no reason. You do not know where you are going or what you intend to do. You can give no definite explanation."

"There is no explanation except that by what I did in Sannet Wood that afternoon I put myself out of touch with human society until I had done something for human society. God has been telling me for many days that I owe a debt. I have tried to avoid paying that debt. I tried to escape Him because I knew that he demanded that I must pay my debt before I could come to you. I see this as clearly as I saw yesterday the high white clouds above the football field. God now is as real to me as you are. It is as though for the rest of my life I must live in a house with two persons. We cannot all live together until certain conditions are granted. I go to make those conditions possible. Because I have broken the law I am an outlaw. I am impelled to win my way back to citizenship again. God will show me."

"But this is air—all nerves. God is nothing. God does not exist."

"God does exist. I must work out His order and then I will come back to you."

She began to be frightened. She caught his coat in her hands, and desperately pleaded. Then she saw his white set face, and the way that his hands gripped the chair, and it was as though she had suddenly found herself alone in the room.

"Olva, don't leave me, don't leave me, Olva. I can't live without you. I don't care what you've done. I'll bear everything with you. I'll come away with you. I'll do anything if only you will let me be with you."

"No, I must go alone."

"But it can't matter—it can't matter. I'm so unimportant. You shall do what you feel is your duty—only let me be there."

"No, I must go alone."

She began to cry, bitter, miserable, sobbing, sitting on the floor, away from him. Her crying was the only sound in the room.

He bent and touched her—"Margaret dear—you make it so hard."

At last, in that strange beautiful way that she had, control seemed suddenly to come to her; she stood up and looked as though she had, in that brief moment, lived a thousand years of sorrow.

"You will come back?"

"I swear that I will come back to you."

"I—I—will—wait for you."

There, in the dim, unreal room, as they had stood once before, now, standing, they were wrapt together. They were very young to feel such depths of tragedy, to touch such heights of beauty. They were a long time there together.

"Margaret darling, you know that I will come back."

"I know that you will come back."

"Olva!"

"Margaret!"

He left her.

Then, standing with outstretched arms, alone there, she who had but now denied the Pursuer, cried to the dark room—

"God, God—send him back to me!"

Some one promised her.

CHAPTER XVII

FIRST CHAPTER

The sun was rising, hard and red, over Sannet Wood and the white frozen flats, when Olva Dune set out.
. . .

Sir Hugh Seymour Walpole, CBE was born in Auckland, New Zealand, on March 13th, 1884.

His parents had moved to New Zealand in 1877, but his mother, Mildred, unable to settle there, eventually persuaded, in 1889, her husband, Somerset, an Anglican clergyman, to accept another post, this time in New York.

Walpole's early years involved being educated by a Governess until, in 1893, his parents decided he needed an English education and the young Walpole was sent to England.

He first attended a preparatory school in Truro. He naturally missed his family but was reasonably happy. A move to Sir William Borlase's Grammar School in Marlow in 1895, found him bullied, frightened and miserable. He later said, "The food was inadequate, the morality was 'twisted', and Terror–sheer, stark unblinking Terror–stared down every one of its passages ... The excessive desire to be loved that has always played so enormous a part in my life was bred largely, I think, from the neglect I suffered there".

In 1896 Somerset Walpole, hearing of his son's unhappiness, moved him to the King's School, Canterbury. For two years he settled but was undistinguished as a pupil. The following year, 1897, Walpole senior was appointed principal of Bede College, Durham, and his son was moved again; to be a day boy for four years at Durham School. Day boys were regarded as the underclass by boarders, and Bede College was the subject of snobbery within the university. His sense of isolation increased. He continually took refuge in the local library, where he read all the novels of Austen, Fielding, Scott and Dickens and many others. He was voracious in reading.

Walpole wrote in 1924: "I grew up ... discontented, ugly, abnormally sensitive, and excessively conceited. No one liked me–not masters, boys, friends of the family, nor relations who came to stay; and I do not in the least wonder at it. I was untidy, uncleanly, excessively gauche. I believed that I was profoundly misunderstood, that people took my pale and pimpled countenance for the mirror of my soul, that I had marvellous things of interest in me that would one day be discovered".

From 1903 to 1906 Walpole studied history at Emmanuel College, Cambridge and there, in 1905, had his first work published, the critical essay "Two Meredithian Heroes". Here he met and fell under the spell of A C Benson. Walpole's religious beliefs, previously sacrosanct, were fading, and Benson helped him through that personal crisis. Walpole was also attempting to cope with his homosexual feelings, which, for a while, focused on Benson.

Benson gently declined Walpole's advances. They remained friends, but Walpole, feeling rebuffed, gradually downgraded the relationship. Two years later Benson's diary entry on Walpole's subsequent social career reveals his thoughts on his protégé's progress: "He seems to have conquered Gosse completely. He spends his Sundays in long walks with H G Wells. He dines every week with Max Beerbohm and R Ross ... and this has befallen a not very clever young man of 23. Am I a little jealous?– no, I don't think so. But I am a little bewildered ... I do not see any sign of intellectual power or perception or grasp or subtlety in his work or himself. ... I should call him curiously unperceptive. He does not, for instance, see what may vex or hurt or annoy people. I think he is rather tactless–though he is himself very sensitive. The strong points about him are his curiosity, his vitality, his eagerness, and the emotional fervour of his affections. But he seems to me in no way likely to be great as an artist.

Somerset Walpole, himself the son of an Anglican priest, hoped that his eldest son would follow him into the ministry. Walpole was concerned for his father's feelings. So much so that on graduation from Cambridge in 1906 he took a post as a lay missioner at the Mersey Mission to Seamen in Liverpool. He described that as one of the "greatest failures of my life". Walpole resigned after six months.

From April to July 1907 Walpole was in Germany, privately tutoring children before returning, in 1908, to teach French at Epsom College.

Walpole now found the desire to fully immerse himself in the literary world. He moved to London to become a book reviewer for The Standard and to write fiction in his spare time. He had by this time come to terms with his homosexuality. His encounters were discreet, as they were illegal in Britain. He was constantly searching for "the perfect friend".

In 1909, Walpole published his first novel, The Wooden Horse, the story of a staid, snobbish English family shaken by the return of one of their own from a more out-going New Zealand. The book received good reviews but sold little.

Better was to come in 1911 when he published Mr Perrin and Mr Traill. The Guardian observed that "the setting of Mr Perrin and Mr Traill was clearly drawn from life". The boys of Epsom College were delighted with the thinly disguised version of their school, but the authorities were not, and Walpole was persona non grata there for many years. It was an early illustration of his capacity, noted by Benson, for unthinkingly giving offence, though being hypersensitive to criticism himself.

In early 1914 Henry James wrote an article for The Times Literary Supplement surveying the younger generation of British novelists and comparing them with their eminent elders. In the latter category James put Bennett, Conrad, Galsworthy, Hewlett and H G Wells. The four new authors were Walpole, Gilbert Cannan, Compton Mackenzie and D H Lawrence. From Walpole's point of view one of the greatest living authors had publicly ranked him among the finest young British novelists.

As war approached, Walpole realised that his poor eyesight would disqualify him from serving in the armed forces. He volunteered for the police, but was turned down. He then accepted an appointment, based in Moscow, reporting for The Saturday Review and The Daily Mail. Although he was allowed to visit the front in Poland, these dispatches were not enough to stop hostile comments at home that he was not doing his bit for the war effort.

Walpole was ready with a counter; an appointment as a Russian officer, in the Sanitar. He explained they were "part of the Red Cross that does the rough work at the front, carrying men out of the trenches, helping at the base hospitals in every sort of way, doing every kind of rough job. They are an absolutely official body and I shall be one of the few Englishmen in the world wearing Russian uniform".

While training Walpole spent many hours gaining fluency in Russian, and writing a literary biography of Joseph Conrad.

In the summer of 1915 he worked on the Austrian-Russian front, assisting at operations in field hospitals and retrieving the dead and wounded from the battlefield. Writing home to Arnold Bennett he said "A battle is an amazing mixture of hell and a family picnic—not as frightening as the dentist, but absorbing, sometimes thrilling like football, sometimes dull like church, and sometimes simply physically sickening like bad fish. Burying the dead afterwards is worst of all."

During a skirmish in June 1915 Walpole rescued a wounded soldier; his Russian comrades refused to help and this meant Walpole had to carry one end of a stretcher, dragging the man to safety. He was awarded the Cross of Saint George.

In October 1915 he returned to England to visit family and friends and to stay at a cottage he had purchased in Cornwall. In January 1916 he was asked by the Foreign Office to return to Petrograd.

Before going his novel, The Dark Forest, was published. It drew on his experiences in Russia, and was more sombre than much of his earlier fiction. Reviews were highly favourable; The Daily Telegraph commented on "a high level of imaginative vision ... reveals capacity and powers in the author which we had hardly suspected before."

Back in Petrograd his diary entry for March 13th records "Thirty two today! Should have been a happy day but was completely clouded for me by reading in the papers of Henry James' death. This was a terrible shock to me."

By late 1917 it was clear to Walpole and the authorities that his work was at an end. On November 7th he left, missing the Bolshevik Revolution, which began that very day.

In London Walpole was appointed to a post at the Foreign Office and remained there until resigning in February 1919. For his wartime work he was awarded the CBE in 1918.

Walpole continued to write and publish and now also began a career on the highly lucrative lecture tour in the United States.

He made his first lecture tour in 1919, receiving an enthusiastic welcome wherever he went. It was noted that Walpole's "genial and attractive appearance, his complete lack of aloofness, his exciting fluency as a speaker and his obvious and genuine liking for his hosts" combined to win him a large American following. The success of his talks led to an increase in lecturing fees, greater sales of his books, and large sums from American publishers keen to print his latest fiction.

A keen music lover, Walpole, in 1920, heard a new tenor at the Proms, impressed he sought him out. Lauritz Melchior became one of the most important friendships of his life, and Walpole did much to foster the singer's budding career. Wagner's son Siegfried engaged Melchior for the Bayreuth Festival in 1924 and succeeding years. Walpole attended, and met Adolf Hitler, then recently released from prison after an attempted putsch.

In 1924 Walpole moved to a house, Brackenburn, near Keswick in the Lake District. His large income enabled him to maintain his London flat in Piccadilly, but Brackenburn was his main home for the rest of his life.

At the end of 1924 Walpole met Harold Cheevers, who soon became his friend and companion and remained so for the rest of his life. Cheevers, a policeman, with a wife and two children, left the police force and entered Walpole's service as his chauffeur. Walpole trusted him completely, and gave him extensive control over his affairs. Whether Walpole was at Brackenburn or Piccadilly, Cheevers was almost always with him, and often accompanied him on overseas trips. Walpole provided a house in Hampstead for Cheevers and his family.

During the mid-twenties Walpole produced two of his best-known novels in the macabre vein that he drew on from time to time, exploring the fascination of fear and cruelty. The Old Ladies (1924) is a study of a timid elderly spinster exploited and eventually frightened to death by a predatory widow. Portrait of a Man with Red Hair (1925) depicts the malign influence of a manipulative, insane father on his family and others.

Walpole continued a series of stories for children, begun in 1919 with Jeremy, taking the young hero's story forward with Jeremy and Hamlet (the boy's dog) in 1923, and Jeremy at Crale in 1927.

In 1930 Walpole wrote possibly his best-known work, Rogue Herries, a historical novel set in the Lake District. The Daily Mail considered it "not only a profound study of human character, but a subtle and intimate biography of a place." He followed it with four sequels and an almost finished fifth.

Hollywood, in the shape of MGM, invited him in 1934 to write the script for a film of David Copperfield. Walpole enjoyed life in Hollywood, but as one who rarely revised any of his work he found it a bore to produce sixth and seventh drafts at the behest of the studio. He also had a small acting role in the film; he played the Vicar of Blunderstone delivering a boring sermon that sends David to sleep.

Walpole's performance was a success. The sermon was improvised and the producer, David O Selznick, had mischievously called for retake after retake to try to make him dry up, but Walpole fluently delivered a different extempore address each time.

The critical and commercial success of the film led to a return in 1936. Arriving, he found the studio had no idea which films they wanted him to work on, and he had eight weeks of highly paid leisure, during which he wrote a short story and worked on a novel. He was eventually asked to write the script for Little Lord Fauntleroy. He spent most of his fees on paintings; he was an avid collector and left many to the Tate in London on his death. His last lecture tour, also in 1936, was primarily to raise funds to pay US taxes which he had neglected to pay earlier.

In 1937 Walpole was offered a knighthood. He accepted although Kipling, Hardy, Galsworthy had all refused. "I'm not of their class... Besides I shall like being a knight," he said.

Walpole's taste for adventure did not diminish in his last years. In 1939 he was commissioned to report for William Randolph Hearst's newspapers on the funeral in Rome of Pope Pius XI, the conclave to elect his successor, and the subsequent coronation. In the weeks between the funeral and Pius XII's election Walpole, with his customary fluency, wrote much of Roman Fountain, a mixture of fact and fiction about the city. It was his last overseas visit.

After the outbreak of the Second World War Walpole remained in England, dividing his time between London and Keswick, where he continued to write with his usual speed. He completed a fifth novel in the Herries series and began work on a sixth.

Unfortunately his health was undermined by diabetes. He overexerted himself at the opening of Keswick's fund-raising "War Weapons Week" in May 1941, making a speech after taking part in a lengthy march.

Sir Hugh Seymour Walpole, CBE died of a heart attack at Brackenburn, aged 57 on June 1st, 1941. He was buried in St John's churchyard in Keswick.

Hugh Walpole – A Concise Bibliography

Books
The Wooden Horse (1909)
Maradick at Forty: A Transition (1910)
Mr Perrin and Mr Traill (1911) (Revised for the US version as The Gods and Mr Perrin)
The Prelude to Adventure (1912)
Fortitude (1913)
The Duchess of Wrexe, Her Decline and Death (1914)
The Golden Scarecrow (Short Stories) (1915)
Prologue
Hugh Seymour
Henry Fitzgeorge Strether
Ernest Henry
Angelina
Bim Rochester
Nancy Ross
'Enery
Barbara Flint
Sarah Trefusis
Young John Scarlet
Epilogue
The Dark Forest (1916)
Joseph Conrad (1916)
The Green Mirror (1918)
The Secret City (1919)
Jeremy (1919)
The Art of James Branch Cabell (1920)
The Captives (1920)
The Thirteen Travellers (Short Stories) (1920)
Absalom Jay
Fanny Close
The Hon Clive Torby
Miss Morganhurst
Peter Westcott
Lucy Moon
Mrs Porter and Miss Allen
Lois Drake

Mr Nix
Lizzie Rand
Nobody
Bombastes Furioso
The Young Enchanted (1921)
The Cathedral (1922)
Jeremy and Hamlet (1923)
The Crystal Box (1924) Privately published by Walpole – limited edition of 150 copies
The Old Ladies (1924)
The English Novel: Some Notes on its Evolution (1924)
Portrait of a Man with Red Hair (1925)
Harmer John (1926)
Reading: An Essay (1926)
Jeremy at Crale (1927)
Anthony Trollope (1928)
My Religious Experience (1928)
The Silver Thorn (Short Stories) (1928)
The Little Donkeys with the Crimson Saddles
The Tiger
No Unkindness Intended
Ecstasy
A Picture
Old Elizabeth (A Portrait)
The Etching
Chinese Horses
The Tarn
Major Wilbraham
A Silly Old Fool
The Enemy
The Enemy in Ambush
The Dove
Bachelors
Wintersmoon (1928)
Farthing Hall (1929) With J B Priestley
Hans Frost (1929)
Rogue Herries (1930)
Above the Dark Circus (1931) Published in the US as Above the Dark Tumult
Judith Paris (1931)
The Apple Trees: Four Reminiscences (1932) Limited edition of 500 copies
The Fortress (1932)
A Letter to a Modern Novelist (1932)
All Souls' Night (Short Stories) 1933
The Whistle
The Silver Mask
The Staircase
A Carnation for an Old Man
Tarnhelm – or The Death of my Uncle Robert
Mr Oddy

Seashore Macabre – A Moment's Experience
Lilac
The Oldest Talland
The Little Ghost
Mrs Lunt
Sentimental but True
Portrait in Shadow
The Snow
The Ruby Glass
Spanish Dusk
Vanessa (1933)
Extracts from a Diary (1934) Privately published by Walpole
Captain Nicholas (1934)
Cathedral Carol Service (1934) An episode from "The Inquisitor"
The Inquisitor (1935)
Claude Houghton: Appreciations (1935) With Clemence Dane
A Prayer for My Son (1936)
John Cornelius: His Life and Adventures (1937)
Head in Green Bronze and Other Stories (1938)
Head in Green Bronze
The German
The Exile
The Train
The Haircut
Let The Bores Tremble
The Honey-Box
The Fear of Death
The Field with Five Trees
Having No Hearts
The Conjurer
The Joyful Delaneys (1938)
The Sea Tower (1939)
Roman Fountain (1940)
The Bright Pavilions (1940)
The Blind Man's House (1941)
Open Letter of an Optimist (1941)
The Killer and the Slain (1942)
Katherine Christian (1943)
Mr Huffam and Other Stories (1948)
The White Cat
The Train to the Sea
The Perfect Close
Service for the Blind
The Faithful Servant
Miss Thom
Women are Motherly
The Beard
The Last Trump

Green Tie
The Church in the Snow
Mr Huffam – A Christmas Story

Editor

In 1932 Walpole edited The Waverley Pageant: Best Passages from the Novels of Sir Walter Scott. In 1937 he edited a compilation of short stories, A Second Century of Creepy Stories (Hutchinson, 1937), by a range of writers including Guy de Maupassant, M. R. James, Henry James, Walter de la Mare, Oliver Onions, Walpole himself ("Tarnhelm") and twenty-one others.